TIDINGS OF COMFORT & JOY

TIDINGS OF COMFORT & JOY

DAVIS BUNN

WestBow
PRESS
A Division of Thomas Nelson Publishers
Since 1798
www.thomasnelson.com

Published in Nashville, Tennessee, by WestBow Press, and distributed in Canada by Word Communications, Ltd., Richmond, British Columbia.

WestBow Publishing books may be purchased in bulk for educational, business, fundraising, or sales promotional use. For information, please e-mail: SpecialMarkets@ThomasNelson.com.

Library of Congress Cataloging-in-Publication Data

Bunn, T. Davis, 1952–
Tidings of comfort and joy / T. Davis Bunn.
p. cm.
ISBN 1-5955-4073-3 (repak)
ISBN 0-7852-7203-8 (hc)
I. Title.
[PS3552.U4718T5 1997b]
813'.54—dc21 97-24436
CIP

Printed in the United States of America.

05 06 07 08 09 QW 9 8 7 6 5 4 3 2 1

To Jack and Jo Ann Bundy

For your guidance and

prayer support over the years,

And most of all

For enriching us with your friendship

ONE

Emily watched her daughter pull the station wagon into the drive. She stood by the twin fir trees, now dressed with Christmas lights. Patches of unmelted snow gave the front lawn a wintry freckled look. She gave her daughter Carol a little wave of greeting, but neither smiled. Before the engine was cut off Emily's two grandsons had already tumbled out, moving as though sprung from ejector seats. Through the wagon's open doors a continual high-pitched wailing could be heard.

Carol walked to where Emily stood in her shapeless cardigan. She kissed her mother's cheek, and said, "I can't believe I'm doing this to you."

"You don't have any choice," Emily replied, her gaze still upon the car. "Your entire family is desperately in need of this vacation."

"Mom, you'll never know how much this means—"

Emily Albright waved it aside. "Let's get this over with," she said, and started toward the car.

"Hello, Gran," George Junior, the elder of the two teenage boys, said. His brother, Buddy, mumbled something that might have been a greeting. But neither could manage to meet their grandmother's eyes.

She gave them both a smile, reached over, and ruffled George Junior's hair. "You've no need to feel guilty, neither one of you."

George resembled his father, with corn-silk hair and eyes like an early dawn sky. He winced at the cries coming from the car. "I wish she could come with us."

"Of course you do. But she can't, and that's that. Don't you worry. We'll have ourselves a grand old time here."

"No, we *won't*," wailed the voice. "I'll *never* have any fun. I'm going to be miserable for the rest of my life!"

"She's been saying that for two days," Buddy said glumly.

"Come along, now. It's getting colder, and the weatherman's predicting snow. We can't just leave her out here."

"That's *exactly* what you're doing!" Through the wagon's side window an unkempt head of honey-brown hair rose into view. Normally Marissa was a buoyant fourteen year old who would never be caught dead in public unless perfectly groomed. Today, however, the car window framed a flushed and tear-streaked face. "You're leaving me and you're going off and you don't love me at *all*. Nobody does. *Nobody* cares about me!"

Emily's smile was gone now. She asked the boys, "Can you two manage her?"

"We got her in," George Junior said.

"But she didn't like it," Buddy added.

"Just be careful, especially on those front stairs. Last week's snow has melted, but they're still wet and slippery."

The two boys walked around to the back of the car, and were greeted with, "Don't you dare *touch* me!"

"I hate it when she talks like that," Buddy mumbled. He was looking nowhere but at his feet. "It's like she blames us for her being sick."

Carol opened the wagon's rear door, which only made the noise louder. The girl lying on the mattress in the back shrilled, "I hope you feel so guilty you shrivel up and die!"

Carol shot a worried glance at her mother, clearly concerned that she was doing the wrong thing. But Emily pointed the two boys forward. "Go on, now. Be careful."

"Come on, Buddy," George urged quietly. "It won't get any better if we wait."

The thin foam mattress had side straps, which the boys grasped and pulled out the back. As the blanket-clad figure came into view, she shouted, "I hope you have the most horrible time you've ever had in your whole rotten lives!"

Her two older brothers refused to look at their sister as they hefted the mattress and sidestepped down the walk. Emily moved in behind them. "Take her to the big bedroom at the top of the stairs."

Marissa flung out a feeble fist, which George Junior easily dodged. "I won't let you do this, I *won't*!"

Emily caught sight of Buddy wincing in pain over the words. She frowned but said nothing.

The two boys carried Marissa into the front hall. Her pitiful wails and her energy were fading fast. By the time they had climbed the stairs, the cries had diminished to frail whimpers. The girl's eyes closed, the tears dried, the moans grew quieter still. The others breathed easier.

As Carol quietly lowered her cases, Emily pulled back the

bedcovers. Together the two women lifted Marissa from the mattress and settled her onto the bed. Emily hesitated a moment before settling the sheet into place. She stared at her granddaughter and murmured, "She's still losing weight."

"Not that much," Carol whispered. "She's just growing so fast, two inches in the past six months. It makes her look skinnier."

"Fourteen is such a difficult age," Emily said, laying the sheet over her.

Carol picked up the quilt she had brought from Marissa's bed, and tucked it in and around her daughter. As she straightened, she found that Marissa's eyes were open and watching her solemnly.

They stood like that for a long moment, mother looking down at daughter, until Marissa's eyes again began to sink shut. With an overly quiet voice, she said, "You don't love me at all, do you, Momma?"

Buddy dropped his side of the empty mattress and fled from the room.

"Oh, darling, darling." Carol reached down and cradled Marissa's face with both hands. "I love you with all my heart, and that is the truth as best I know how to say it."

George pulled the mattress over to the doorway, stopped, and said quietly, "I'll miss you, Sis. Merry Christmas."

Marissa struggled to keep her eyes opened and fastened upon her mother. "Why is everybody going away and leaving me alone, Momma?"

"I would do anything if I could be lying there instead of

you," Carol said, and a single tear escaped to trace its way down her cheek. But her daughter did not see it. Marissa's eyes had defeated her best efforts and closed on their own accord.

Carol sat there and stroked Marissa's face, then rose to her feet with a weary sigh. She turned to her mother and said quietly, "I don't know if I can let you do this."

"We'll be fine," Emily said.

But this time Carol was going to have it out and said, "This will be your first Christmas without Dad. You don't need this."

"I'm not so sure about that," Emily responded quietly.

Carol was too busy with her own worries to hear her mother. "You've been talking about this Indiana reunion for over a month. I hate to see you miss it on our account."

"She needs me, Carol. All those families can be seen another time."

Carol felt defeat crowding in. She tried once more with, "You've seen how she is, Mom."

"Yes. And I also see how tired you are. All of you. It's been an exhausting year for everyone. George's company almost going under, then my Colin passing on, now Marissa's illness." Emily's tone was flat and determined. "You have to go. We've been through this a dozen times. You *have* to. This vacation has been like a lifeline for all of you."

Carol's shoulders slumped. She rubbed her forehead, her cheek, the back of her neck. "I'm so tired I can't even think straight anymore."

Emily gave her a fierce hug, turned her around, and guided her out of the room and back down the stairs. "Go and start getting ready for the time of your lives."

At the front door, Carol halted once more. "Are you really sure about this, Mom?"

"I am," Emily replied calmly. "Who knows, this may turn out to be a blessing in disguise."

TWO

Marissa awoke to the smell of soup. She opened her eyes. Her grandmother had pulled a chair up close to the bed and was sipping from a steaming cup. "Good evening. Are you hungry?"

Reluctantly she nodded. She hated her body. She hated how it kept her trapped in this bed and in this house. She hated how it had grown until she looked like she was nothing but a scarecrow, her clothes flapping on empty sticks. And now she hated how it refused to let her just lie in misery, how it forced her to wake up to a world she hated, and made her hungry for food she didn't want. "What time is it?"

"Almost eight. You've slept over twelve hours." The edges of Gran's eyes crinkled with the tiniest of smiles, one that did not touch her mouth at all. "That little tantrum of yours must have tired you out. It certainly did me."

Marissa blushed at her grandmother's matter-of-fact tone. The way she said the words made her feel even worse. "They've gone off and left me," she said morosely.

"Yes, they did." There was no getting around the directness in Gran's voice. "Carol called from the airport about an hour ago. They were just boarding the plane.

She'd been waiting to see if she could speak with you again, but I told her not to bother. I said you needed time to get used to the way things are."

"The way things are is just plain awful," Marissa declared. She felt another flare of anger over being left behind. But then she recalled how she had screamed at her brothers, and how sad Buddy had looked. The anger mingled with shame, pinching her heart. She had always been so close to Buddy.

Marissa found herself hoping that her grandmother would disagree, so that she could use the renewed anger to push back her shame.

Yet all Gran said was, "Thing are indeed truly awful. But they could also be far worse."

"I don't see how," Marissa muttered crossly. Yet the remorse still flickered like shadows just beyond the light's reach.

"Shall I help you sit up so you can have some soup?" When Marissa nodded, Gran set down her cup, rose, and helped her slide up in bed. As she plumped the pillows behind her granddaughter's back, she went on, "Well, let's see. At least we know you're going to get better."

"They haven't even told me what's the matter," Marissa said glumly.

"Yes they have. A little, anyway. But you weren't listening."

"They keep treating me like a child."

"Well, that's partly because you've been acting like one. Here." Gran handed her a mug. "Homemade chicken soup. Good for what ails you." She watched Marissa take a tentative sip, and went on, "Your folks also didn't tell you much because there was a lot they weren't sure of. Which was why they've been so scared."

"Scared? Of what?"

"Of you dying." Gran watched Marissa with that calm stare of hers. "They thought you had leukemia."

A cold wind passed over Marissa's heart. "That's what all those tests were about?"

"Some of them. The doctors couldn't figure out why you were so tired all the time," Gran replied. "So they started eliminating one possible ailment after another. And all the while there was that terrible fear at the back of their minds."

"Leukemia," Marissa said, and sipped again. "I've heard of that. It's bad, isn't it?"

"Horrible. As bad as bad can be. It's a child killer of the first degree."

Over the rim of her mug, Marissa regarded the older woman. Her grandmother had changed a lot in that year since Granpa had died. He had passed on just after Christmas of the year before, a time that had been hard for all of them. The frank way her grandmother observed her now, the way she seemed ready to sit and wait there forever, gave her the strength to say, "It seems like the whole world has come unwound since Granpa died."

Gran backed off a notch, clearly caught off guard. Marissa took a little pleasure in that, being able to make somebody else hurt. But the feeling was instantly replaced by a pang of guilt. Her grandmother watched her with a gaze that seemed keen enough to understand exactly what was going on inside her, but all Gran said was, "Well, mine sure did."

The pain inside Marissa seemed to grow even stronger. But her words seemed to come of their own accord. "You've gotten a lot thinner. And you cut off your long hair. And you've gotten, I don't know, harder. No, that's not the word."

"I think I understand," Gran said, and set down her cup. "I've lost some of my sweetness, haven't I? All my soft edges have gotten sharper."

The quiet way she spoke those words made Marissa feel so ashamed. "I'm sorry, Gran. I didn't—"

"Shah, child. There's no need to apologize." She took one of Marissa's hands in both of hers. "You are absolutely right. I'm sure everyone else has noticed and thinks about it, but they just don't want to say anything. I can't help it, you see. I lived for my Colin. He was the center of my world. And now he's gone."

There was a little lilt to that last sentence, so much longing that it pulled up the edges of the words. Gran gave a big sigh, as though trying to push all the pain back inside her chest. She raised sorrowful eyes to Marissa's, and went on. "I've had to pare things down to their very essentials. That's what it takes at a time like this, just to keep going."

Marissa wasn't sure she understood what Gran had said, but she heard the emotion behind the words. "You miss Granpa a lot, don't you?"

"With every breath. With every thought. With every passing minute."

Until that very moment it had never occurred to Marissa that romance was something people as old as Gran could feel. But the way Gran said those words, and the way she turned to look up and out the window, searching the night for a man who was no longer there, made Marissa's heart swell with a shared sorrow. "I miss him too."

"I know you do, child." Gran did not turn back from the window. "We all do. He was a truly wonderful man."

But it was not missing Granpa that bound Marissa to her grandmother at that moment. "Now we both have a reason to hate Christmas," she said.

That brought Gran around. "What a thing to say." There was no anger to her voice, no criticism. Just a quiet surprise. "I don't hate Christmas."

"But you . . ." Then it came, the blanket of sleep rising so swiftly that she would have spilled soup all over herself had Gran not reached out and taken hold of the mug. "Oooh."

"You sleep, child," Gran whispered. She set down the mug, leaned over, and kissed Marissa's closed eyes. "You sleep."

IN THE NIGHT'S darkest hour, Marissa awoke with a strangled cry.

"Shah, child, it's all right." Gran was instantly there beside her. "It was only a dream."

She rose from the depths of lingering fatigue with great effort. The edges of the nightmare clung to her like tentacles. "It was horrible."

"Everything is fine." Gran settled on the edge of her bed, and stroked the sweat-limp hair from her forehead. "Don't worry about a thing."

"I was back in the doctor's office. He had a needle. It looked two feet long. And thick as Daddy's drill." She shuddered at the memory. "He was going to stick it in me."

A streetlight shone through the frosted windowpane, the yellowish tint making Gran's features look old. And determined. "Nobody is going to examine you with any more needles. Of that you can be sure."

"But I remember something." It was hard to tell the difference between what was a dream and what was real. Yet there was a hint of memory hidden in the shadows. "Sometime when I was in a doctor's office, did you and Momma quarrel?"

Gran's fingers hesitated a moment. "I hoped you had slept through all that. You were conked out on the examining table. I shouldn't have let my voice rise so."

It was comforting to sit there, to feel the gentle caress, to know that she shared the night with someone who cared for her, who would protect her always. "I can't remember you and Momma ever quarreling before. That's why I was sure it was a dream."

"I was not quarreling with your mother. It was that doctor. That's whom I was angry with." A spark of annoyance returned to Gran's voice. "They had eliminated almost every possibility. But he still wanted to continue with those silly tests of his."

Marissa clutched at the covers. "There *was* a needle, wasn't there? A *big* one. That wasn't a dream at all."

"He wanted to do a liver biopsy, which required taking a sample of your liver tissue. Of all the . . ." Gran stopped and gathered herself. "You had become slightly jaundiced. That means your skin had turned a little yellow. And your liver had swollen up so I could feel it with my own fingers. Anyone with any sense would know what was ailing you. But that doctor, he kept saying the tests weren't conclusive. Just this one last test—he must have said those words a dozen times. Shooting us off to the hospital and the clinic and back to his office again, making everybody worry until the results came back, and then saying we had to go through it again. Just one more time. Over and over, without end."

Marissa drew the covers up close to her chin. She could feel the tendrils of fear all the way down to her toes. "He was going to stick a big needle through my tummy and into my liver?"

"Nobody is going to do anything to you, child. I promise you." Gran resumed her gentle stroking. "Would you like an old woman's diagnosis of what's wrong with you?"

"Yes." Her voice sounded tiny to her own ears.

"You have hepatitis. A strain they haven't identified yet. I've seen it in children before. And I've talked to some other doctors since all this started. There are several new strains around, some they're just beginning to recognize. These don't show up on the regular tests. But there is no cure for hepatitis except rest. So having them jab you with another needle would do nothing except satisfy the doctor's curiosity. That way, if he can't heal you, at least he can feel professional by putting a name to your illness."

"Momma was going to let him do it?"

"Your mother has been pulled in so many different directions recently, she's lucky she can remember her own name. As soon as I started arguing with the doctor, though, she saw the light of day. Carol was the one who told the doctor we'd had enough. Not me."

Marissa lay there a long moment, coming to grips with a nightmare that had almost happened. She glanced around the room, and saw that Gran had made up a rollaway bed in the corner. The sight was very comforting. "How did you know about, what was that name?"

"Hepatitis." For some reason, the question brought a smile to Gran's features. "Oh, child, that is a long, long story."

"Tell me."

"I wouldn't even know where to begin. Telling you that story would be like pulling at a thread. Once I start, the whole thing would just unravel in my hands."

"But I want to hear."

The gentle fingers stroking her temples communicated a quiet message of their own. One that spoke to her body and not her mind, whispering a message of comfort, inviting the sleep to come back up and recapture her. Gran said softly, "I'll think about it."

Marissa gave a mighty yawn. "Why am I so sleepy all the time, Gran?"

"That's what an illness of the liver does to your body. It makes things slow down, so that it can repair itself. You need to rest just as much as you can."

Marissa started to say that she would sleep some more, and that she was glad Gran was there with her in the night, and a lot of other things, but the words were swept up and away, like leaves swirled away by a strong winter breeze. The last thing Marissa knew was the touch of Gran's gentle fingers on her forehead.

THREE

Marissa dreamed she heard the telephone ringing. She awoke to hear Gran talking to someone who was not there. Something in the tone told her it was her mother, even before the words became clear. Instantly the heartache was back, and with it the anger.

"Hang on, I'll see if she's awake." Gran tapped on the door, pushed it open. She held the portable phone to her ear. She gave Marissa a smile, and said, "It's your mother."

Marissa gave her head a fierce little shake. "I don't want to talk with her."

Marissa half-expected Gran to tell her mother to hold on, then come in and argue with her, ordering her to say something. Which she would, of course, sulking over the phone, trying to make everybody over there feel as bad as she did being trapped here.

But Gran did nothing of the sort. Her stare did not change, but the smile disappeared. In the matter-of-fact tone they had all come to know well over the past year, she said to the phone, "She's not quite over the trauma yet, honey. But I noticed some cracks in the wall last night. Yes, she woke and we had a nice chat. No, I wouldn't force things just now. Yes, of course I'll tell her. Okay. Give my love to the boys. 'Bye."

The phone peeped when Carol cut the connection. Gran said quietly, "Your mother says to tell you that she loves you very much, and she misses you terribly."

"They're there, aren't they?" Marissa said glumly.

"Checked into the hotel, had a shower and a nap, and were getting ready to go exploring." Gran held to her matter-of-fact tone. "Do you think you could come downstairs for breakfast? You need to move around some. It will help shorten the recovery time."

"I guess so."

"Do you need me to help?"

"No, I want to do it myself." Determinedly she pushed herself upright, and swung her legs to the floor. She was very glad that Gran remained standing in the doorway, watching carefully, ready to rush over if she needed help. Her legs were wobbly, but they kept her upright.

Gran stood there until she was certain Marissa could move about on her own. "I laid out a fresh nightie for you in the bathroom. Call me when you get to the top landing. I don't want you to try the stairs on your own just yet."

The lack of criticism and argument left Marissa feeling very unsettled. She found she could not remain angry if there was nothing to react against. And without anger, the pain of her situation seemed even worse, as though by being angry she had escaped from some of the sadness. And the guilt.

Marissa kept one hand on the wall as she entered the

bathroom. It helped to steady herself, which was good, because the weakness was accompanied by a strange dizziness, as though the world was only partly in focus. When she turned on the bathroom light, she groaned aloud at the sight of her face in the mirror. How could she look so tired when all she did was sleep? She had deep circles under her eyes, her hair was matted and tangled, and her cheeks looked sunken.

The process of washing and changing and being helped down the stairs and into the kitchen left Marissa feeling both better and extremely tired. When she was settled at the kitchen table, with Gran's quilted robe wrapped tightly around her, she admitted to herself for the very first time that she could not have made the trip to Hawaii. For some reason, the admission made her pain even worse.

"It was my idea," she gloomily told her grandmother. "To go to Hawaii, I mean. I was the one who thought up the trip."

Gran stopped her moving about the kitchen, and turned to look across the counter. "I know it was, child."

"I saw the ad when Daddy was going through all that awful stuff at the company. He was coming home so late. And he was getting up early. I remember waking up a lot of times while it was still dark and hearing his car pull out of the driveway."

Gran filled a pot with water and set it on the stove to boil. "He was exhausted. For a while he thought the company was going under, and they would all lose their jobs. I was afraid he was working himself into an early grave."

"He looked so tired all the time," Marissa agreed. "But things got better, didn't they?"

"They did indeed. Finally."

"I remember the day he told Momma at the dinner table that he thought they would make it after all. That's when I found the ad. It was in the Sunday paper. A trip to Hawaii for Christmas. A special low-price offer, but we had to book right then, 'cause there were only a few seats. The whole family could go, and it was a hotel and the flights and meals and a car and everything."

"Your mother said it was a miracle, your finding that ad," Gran said. "They couldn't believe how inexpensive it was. Planning that holiday gave everyone a lifeline, something they could look forward to."

"When Momma and Daddy talked about it that night, it was the first time Daddy had smiled in a long long time," Marissa said, remembering. "I felt so proud."

"It was a wonderful thing you did," Gran agreed. "Would you like some oatmeal and maybe some hot chocolate afterward?"

"Okay." But the burning lump of disappointment was so great, she was not sure she could fit food around it.

"I'll have it ready in a jiffy." Gran started moving around the room in her brisk way. "Would you like brown sugar, cinnamon, and raisins?"

Marissa nodded. "Hawaii. I've been dreaming about going there ever since I was little."

"I know you have." Gran measured out a cup of oatmeal, poured it into the boiling water, and stirred briskly.

"I remember when you were young, you loved to make yourself necklaces of flowers using daisies and daffodils. Then you would sing to yourself and do those swaying little dances all around the house. Mmmm, doesn't that cinnamon smell good?"

"I collected pictures of the islands, and learned all the names, and had a book of the flowers." Talking about it only made the disappointment worse. But she couldn't stop. The pain was a balloon in her chest, forcing out the words with its burning pressure. "I used to dream about going out in one of those canoes with the big side float; they're called outriggers. And seeing the coral with all the fish. I wanted to go in one of the glass-bottom boats and study them, and maybe take diving lessons."

Gran brought over two steaming bowls and set one in front of Marissa. "While you were still very little, I remember taking you to your swimming lessons one day. You told me you had to learn to swim very well."

"And dive," Marissa said, blowing on her spoonful.

"That's right, and dive. Because you were going to go to Hawaii. You were going to learn to scuba. I remember how amazed I was that you even knew the word. You were going to take Buddy out to the coral reefs and show him all the pretty fish."

Buddy. Marissa kept spooning the oatmeal into her mouth. Her body had to be fed. But hearing her brother's name brought out such regret that she totally lost her appetite. She had been close to Buddy since she was a baby. The family told stories of how her first smile had been for the middle brother, her first word his name. Buddy was the one always there for her. Marissa found herself recalling what she had said to him the previous day. Her remorse made the oatmeal taste like mud.

Now he was in Hawaii without her. She could not stop thinking about everything she had wanted to do. And how excited she had been when her mom and dad decided to go ahead and book the trip. "We got the last five seats," Marissa whispered, her thoughts about Buddy all muddled with her pain over not being there with them. "That's what the travel agent told Daddy."

Gran set down her spoon, leaned over, and murmured, "Child, do you realize you're crying?"

Marissa set down her spoon. "It's just so unfair. So *bad*."

"This must be so hard for you." She rose from her chair, helped Marissa get up, and led her into the living room. "Look, I've made up the sofa into a little bed. That way you can spend your days down here with me, and I'll decorate the tree right over there, and we'll have a big fire. Won't that be nice?"

As soon as she saw the bed, Marissa felt the rising weakness, as though it had been there the whole time, just waiting for her. The tears stopped. She no longer had the strength to cry, or even to feel enough to *want* to cry. What difference did it make anyway, they were there and she was here, no matter how many tears she shed. "It's all wrong, Gran. It's not supposed to be like this."

"I know, dear. I know."

Marissa allowed her grandmother to take off the robe, guide her down into the bed, and tuck the sheet and blanket up around her. "This can't be a very nice Christmas for you either."

"There's no place I would rather be," Gran replied quietly. "And that's the truth."

Another wave of fatigue hit her. She did not want to give into it, though, not yet. "Didn't Momma say something about a reunion? Or did I dream that?"

"Oh." Gran waved it away as unimportant. "Your Uncle Hank and Aunt Annique had invited me over for Christmas. They were planning a reunion so that I could see the new babies."

Hank was not his real name. Nor was he Marissa's real uncle. In fact, if she understood things correctly, all those families were no relation to her at all. Uncle Hank had a truly impossible last name, something with two *y*'s and a *k*, she remembered that much. He and Aunt Annique had come to visit them once years ago. They had stayed with Gran and Granpa, and seemed to be all smiles the whole time they were around. They both spoke with accents, but not the same as how Granpa used to sound. Harsher. Hank and Annique shared something special with her grandparents, but Marissa wasn't exactly sure what. Something about them both being adopted because of her. Marissa had found that very strange, because they lived outside Indianapolis, and when Marissa had asked her grandparents when they had lived in Indiana, they had all laughed loud and long.

"They didn't want me to be alone this first Christmas without Colin, that's all," her grandmother was saying. "When they heard you were all going to Hawaii, they invited me to come and visit. The reunion can wait. They're not going anywhere, and the babies will only get bigger so there's more to hold."

There were hundreds of them out there in Indiana, Marissa knew that much, and more of them all the time. Most of them were total strangers, people she had never even met. But they all held some special secret bond with her grandparents. They wrote Gran all the time, big long letters full of pictures that Gran framed and hung on the hallway going back to the kitchen. The walls were floor-to-ceiling pictures of families and children and teenagers. Marissa did not know even half their names.

Sleep crept up her frame, inch by inch, a numbing tingle that could not be denied, no matter how hard she fought. "You stayed here because of me?"

Gran gave her a smile, and a hint of the old tenderness returned to her features. Marissa looked up, and saw the way Gran had been before Granpa died, and wondered sleepily why Gran had buried that expression with her grandfather.

"No," Gran said quietly. "I stayed because of *us*."

FOUR

This sleep was not like normal slumber. When Marissa awoke, she felt as though it was still with her, a shadow just at the edge of the room, always ready to come back and sweep her away unless she was very careful and very alert.

Something else was different about this fatigue. She would sleep, and when she awoke, it felt as if no time at all had passed. She found it hard to believe the clock's message that four or five or eight or fourteen hours were gone from her life. She felt as though she had just closed her eyes, and then opened them again.

Thoughts that she had started the last time she was awake, or even the time before that, still seemed new. As though her mind had come to a complete halt when she closed her eyes. Marissa found it very frightening, how all her inside world seemed to just stop whenever she gave in to this tiredness. Each sleep had the taste of a small death, and for the first time she was forced to realize that she was human, that she would someday pass away.

Marissa tried to move her mind off those worries.

She lay on the little sofa bed and watched as Gran hung

glittering balls and tiny angels on the Christmas tree. Gran was working as quietly as she could, but every once in a while she would hum a single note, as though she was listening to music in her mind, and occasionally a bit of it would break out.

Marissa said, "I forgot about how you and Granpa celebrated your wedding anniversary at Christmas."

"Not exactly our anniversary, but we did like to have a private little party around Christmastime." She smiled over at Marissa. "I didn't know you were awake. Did you have a nice nap?"

She nodded. "It wasn't your anniversary?"

"No, dear. Colin and I were married in June. The twenty-first of June, the first day of summer." She hung up another shimmering bauble. "Why were you wondering about that, dear?"

"You know, what we talked about this morning. Why you don't hate Christmas."

"Oh. I see." Gran sat down on the floor beside the tree and gave it some thought. "I suppose what Colin and I shared does have a little to do with how I feel about the season. A little. But not a lot."

"I guess I don't understand," Marissa said, the words carried upon a very soft sigh.

Gran remained where she was, her gray eyes regarding Marissa, probing. "I wonder," she finally said, "whether you are old enough to hear about this."

Despite herself, Marissa's interest was instantly piqued. "About what?"

"What we've been dancing around ever since you arrived." Gran pressed both hands on the floor and pushed herself upright. "Let me go see if I can find them."

"Find what, Gran?"

"Wait there, I'll be right back."

But she was not so swift in returning. There was a lot of bumping around overhead, and footsteps going from room to room, before Marissa heard her grandmother exclaim, "There they are! I *knew* I hadn't thrown them out."

When she reappeared, Gran held yellowed squares of paper clasped up close to her chest. She seated herself on the edge of the sofa, and inspected Marissa with the oddest expression Marissa had ever seen. She was very grave, but there was a mischievous light to her eyes. "If I am going to tell you this story, I am going to have to do it as one adult to another."

Marissa scrambled up so that she was more seated than lying. "All right, Gran."

"You haven't been acting very adultlike these past few days," Gran pointed out.

"But I—"

"Never mind." She patted Marissa's arm for silence. "Now there's something more before we begin. This is a precious thing, what I'm about to tell you. Some people know parts of this story, but very few know it all. I'm not even sure if your mother is aware of everything."

As she spoke, Gran grew ever more somber. Her gaze seemed to open up, bigger and bigger, until it seemed as though those two gray eyes filled Marissa's vision. "So I want you to promise me that what I give you is for you alone. You can't tell another person, not as long as I'm alive. This is *my* story, an important part of *my* life. You have to promise me that you will respect this."

Marissa felt a little shiver course through her. Whether it was fear or anticipation she was not sure. "All right, Gran."

"You promise that what we talk about here will remain just between the two of us?"

"I promise."

"Very well, then." There was an instant's hesitation, not as though Gran was still uncertain whether she should act or not, but rather as though a huge old door were opening somewhere just out of sight. And the act of pushing at the long-disused door took so much effort, it had to be done slowly. "I suppose," Gran said quietly, "one of the reasons I've never talked about this before was because I didn't need to, so long as Colin was still with me. But now . . ."

Another instant's hesitation, and Marissa found herself holding her breath. Then Gran unfolded the arm that held the squares of paper, slowly bringing them out and around, until she settled the first one in Marissa's lap. "This is where my story begins."

It was a photograph. A very old one, too, Marissa knew that immediately. The edges were crinkle-cut, and the borders were yellowed. But despite the fading of time, nothing could disguise the attractiveness of the man who smiled up at her. "Who is *that?*"

"His name is Grant Rockwell. Or was. I don't know if he is still alive."

"Wow. He looks like a movie star."

"Isn't that remarkable. Do you know, that was exactly what I thought the first time I saw him. He looked like Clark Gable. More like Clark Gable than Clark Gable himself."

Marissa examined the man. He was wearing a uniform of some sort. His teeth were perfectly even, and his eyes were staring at her with an electric force that made her fingers tingle where they touched the photograph. "He's a hunk."

Her grandmother laughed aloud. "I'm not sure I would use that term, but I share the sentiment. He was the most handsome man I had ever set eyes on."

"But who *is* he?"

"He was a pilot in the American Army Air Corps." The mischievous light had returned to Gran's eyes. "And he was the man I was engaged to marry."

Marissa frowned in concentration. "But Gran, that's not—"

"I said I *was* engaged to marry." She turned her head so as to better see the photograph. "But this was the man I traveled all the way to England for."

A tremor shivered the world upon which Marissa's life was built. "But I thought you went over to meet Granpa."

"That is what we have always told people, and we firmly believe it to be the truth. I was brought across the Atlantic because I was intended to marry the Reverend Colin Albright." The light in her eyes drifted south, lifting the edges of her mouth. "But first the dear Lord had to find some reason to pluck me up and carry me across the ocean, didn't He?"

"I guess so." Granpa was English, Marissa had always known that. He had the nicest way of speaking, not at all like anyone else she knew. He had a very deep voice, and it seemed as though he sang the words instead of just speaking them. She also knew that Gran had left Philadelphia and traveled to England, and met Granpa in a little village where he was preaching. Then they had decided to come back to America.

She didn't know why she found this news of another romance in Gran's past so unsettling. Nonetheless, Marissa knew she wanted to enter through the open door, and walk the dusty lanes of past times and adventures with her grandmother. "Why didn't you marry him?"

"That, my dear, is where our story begins. Here, you might as well see this one, too, before I begin." She set the second photograph in Marissa's lap. "I'm not sure I ever showed that one to Carol."

Marissa found herself blushing without understanding exactly why. A very attractive young woman was leaning forward, her arms wrapped around the handsome man in uniform. He was facing the camera instead of her, so that she leaned against his right side, and he held her with one arm. He gave the camera a jaunty smile. But what shocked Marissa was the woman's expression. She stared up at the man with an eagerness so strong it was almost a hunger. She used both arms to hold him close, and clearly she saw nothing at all except the man she was holding. "Is that you?"

"What a question. Of course it is. Don't you recognize me?"

"I'm not sure." She could see the features belonged to her grandmother. But the look on this woman's face was so strange, so different from anything she had ever known, that Marissa was almost afraid to admit it, even to herself. "I guess so."

Gran took back the pictures, looked long at the one where she held the man, and said softly, "I was a fool in love. There is no other way to explain how I could leave a good job and a nice home and wonderful folks, and sail across the sea in 1945. Which is exactly what I did, less than six months after the war against Germany ended. I left everything I knew, and sailed for a place where I didn't know a soul. And the only reason was, I was crazy in love with a man I scarcely knew."

Marissa gave a delicious little shiver. In those few short sentences were a thousand questions, all of them exciting. She hoped her grandmother would not notice her reaction, for fear that she might stop talking.

Gran's eyes remained fastened upon the photographs. "I left behind a good job in Philadelphia. I had been assistant to the president of the city's largest shipping company. During the war years, a lot of jobs had opened up to women for the first time. I had enjoyed the challenge of organizing a big company's daily operations. We were sending supplies all over the world, which was how I had met Grant Rockwell.

"Grant was a pilot, working with the Lend-Lease programs. He flew American-made planes to all sorts of places—Russia and England mostly. He would come in every couple of weeks, sign the papers, pick up a load of whatever was to be delivered with the plane, and fly off again. Every girl in the office was a little in love with him. Which made it all the sweeter when he fell for me. Or said he did.

"Every time Grant came through he invited me out. It was so exciting in those tense war-filled days to have a dashing pilot arrive and sweep me away. Grant took me to the finest restaurants and to dances and on moonlit . . ."

She stopped then, and seemed to refocus on the room and her granddaughter. What she saw made her pause and say, "Perhaps we should wait until you have rested before we continue."

"I'm fine, Gran." Which was not quite a fib. Marissa felt tired all the time. But she was not sleepy. Her mind was reeling from what she had just learned, but she eagerly wanted more. "Will you talk just a little longer now?"

Marissa's words seemed to strengthen her grandmother's resolve. "If you like. But not too much. Let me start by telling you the reason I have decided to share this secret with you. It is because I, too, have lost a Christmas."

"What do you mean, 'lost'?"

"Exactly what I said, just exactly as you feel you have right now. And I was so heartbroken I didn't want to go on. I thought my life was over."

Her hand reached over to pat Marissa's side, as though

it had taken on a life of its own, for clearly Gran's mind was elsewhere. "But I tell you this with the absolute certainty of having built a life upon the result. That loss was the greatest thing that ever happened to me. It taught me that some lessons can only come to us in the guise of sadness. Some of our greatest gifts start in ways that will tempt us to turn away from what is being offered. But if we have the strength and the will and the faith to accept the bad with the good, we can be rewarded with a richness that is truly beyond human understanding."

Gran continued to pat the blanket, gathering herself for the act of returning to another place and time. When she resumed speaking, her voice altered, softened, became almost lyrical with the power of her memories. "My story really begins four days before the Christmas that never was."

FIVE

GRAN'S STORY

I arrived in England on the twenty-first of December, 1945. Our eleven-day Atlantic crossing had seemed to go on forever. The weather had been simply terrible. The boat was a former troop carrier and now part of a convoy sending over emergency supplies. My cabin had not been much bigger than a closet, with a shower that didn't work. I had suffered from seasickness for five endless days, and in my delirium I had often dreamed that I was caught in a horrible tossing metal prison, and that neither the storm nor the journey would ever end. My guilt over the way I had left home made things much, much worse.

The aid convoy carried everything imaginable, from lightbulbs to shoes. Our particular ship was full to the brim with food, even the empty passenger cabins. The room next to mine contained bananas. I know, because by the fourth day of the trip the fruit had become overripe. The smell only worsened my nausea.

Finally on the seventh day, I started to feel as if I might survive. I was weak as a kitten, not having eaten much, and whatever I had eaten had not stayed down very long. When

I emerged from my cabin, the captain and the chef were in the doorway beside mine, horrified over the sight of four hundred pounds of rotting bananas. That evening, after I had forced down a dinner that still did not sit very easy, the chef served us huge portions of banana cream pie for dessert. The sight almost made me sick all over again.

I recovered from seasickness only to come down with the most horrid cold. Almost everyone on board was caught in its throes. It settled in my lungs, and sapped what little strength I had. The illness was still with me upon our arrival in England.

That morning I joined all the other passengers to watch our entrance into Portsmouth. No one spoke as the tugs pulled us through the harbor mouth and down the long line of quays. We stood there in absolute silence, except for the hacking and wheezing from those who had not yet recovered. My own cough sounded worst of all, but no one paid me any notice. We were too busy absorbing our first glimpse of England through the wind and snow.

The light was bad, very shadowy, so all I could make out were dim silhouettes. The port area had been bombed to smithereens by the Germans. Now the docks were filled with boats, most of them warships. They were in terrible condition. The sides of the vessels and the cannons and the huge smokestacks were blackened by layers of soot. Many of the decks had been torn apart by explosions. Huge metal sheets had been used to repair the worst damage, the work done in such haste that the steel had not even been painted over, just slapped into place before the ships were sent out again. They looked absolutely exhausted, those ships. As if they had barely managed to limp home after the fighting had stopped.

I walked down the gangplank in the face of a bitter wind. A frozen mist too fine to be called snow buffeted me with the force of gritty sand. I stepped onto the harbor road, craning and searching, hoping desperately that Grant would suddenly appear and sweep me up in his strong arms, and tell me that everything was truly all right.

But he was not there. Somehow I made my way to the train station, thankful that the sleet and rain masked my tears. The ticket agent was very kind, but I had the hardest time understanding him. I knew we were speaking the same language, but his words were so strangely spoken, I could not make out a thing.

"What seems to be the matter, luv?"

I turned to a portly woman whose red face beamed up at me. "I just want to buy a ticket." Rather than risk not being understood, I handed over a card that held Grant's address.

"Arden-on-Thames," she said, and smiled. "Ooh, that is a nice spot, from what I hear. Oxfordshire, ain't it?"

"I-I'm not—"

"Yeah, that's it. Nice place. Or was. War years have rubbed away a lot of the polish, that'd be my guess." She was a hefty woman, almost a foot shorter than me and very solid. She wore a black-lacquered hat with bright blue feathers, and they jumped about as she jerked a thumb at the man behind the counter. "This gentleman can only give you a ticket as far as London, dearie. Once you arrive there, you'll need to take a transom to Paddington Station, and buy your ticket onward."

"I'm sorry, take a what?"

"Transom, luv. A cab." She turned to the agent and said, "Just make out the ticket, Bert. I'll see her to the train."

"Right you are." He made a noisy process of filling out the form and stamping it. "That'll be seven and sixpence."

I fumbled with my purse, having no idea what to give the man, until the woman reached in and pried out the required amount. She scooped up the ticket, hefted one of my bags, and led me through the crowd. "Platform seven. You're in luck, dearie. The trains are running close enough to time today. Sort of makes up for the weather."

She clucked sympathetically as another paroxysm of coughing bent me almost double. "You'll need to watch that cold, dearie. It's the weather, mind. Hardest winter on record, and getting worse. Are you just over from the Colonies?"

"No, I'm American."

For some reason, the woman found that deliciously funny. "Oh, I'm glad I ran into you today, I am. It does a body good to have a reason for a chuckle." She set down the case and handed me the ticket. "Here you are, luv. Platform seven. Have a lovely stay in Arden. And a Merry Christmas to you."

I thanked her as well as I could manage, and felt bereft when the woman turned and walked away. It was as though

I had just made and lost my only friend in the whole world.

The train ride was almost as bad as the boat. The carriage was terrifically crowded. Soldiers and sailors crammed into every free inch of space. They smoked and played cards and talked. The air was so thick with tobacco fumes I could have cut it with a knife. None of the windows opened, and a few miles outside the station they fogged up so I could not see a thing. A couple of the sailors tried to chat with me, but quickly gave up. I sat crammed into the hard wooden seat, sadder than I had ever been in my life.

I shut my eyes and tried to rest. At least it eased my coughing, and kept me from being bothered by all the young men. But all the questions seemed to wait and pounce just as soon as I closed my eyes. What was I doing here? What had I gotten myself into? Worse still, what would Grant say when he saw me? I had no answers to any of them. I sat and rocked with the train, and recalled all the events that had brought me to this place.

My parents had never liked Grant Rockwell the least little bit. They thought he was fast—that was how they described a man like Grant back in those days. Fast and dangerous. I thought he was the most exciting man I had ever laid eyes on. He was a happy-go-lucky sort, carefree and full of adventure. When he had started showing special attention to me, I couldn't believe my luck.

Grant came back for New Year's Eve, 1944. It was an exciting time. Victory was in the air. Our boys were pushing hard, and they were rolling back the enemy on almost every front. We went to a party that night, and when we stepped out on the balcony for some air, Grant asked me to marry him.

I felt as if I was walking on air. Little old me, fiancée to the most dashing man any of my girlfriends had ever seen. But my parents were furious. I was still living at home, of course, that's what good girls did in those days until they were married. They went at me tooth and nail, ordering me to break it off, warning that a relationship with Grant would only end in sorrow. I refused, of course. I was quite a hardheaded young lady.

Even after the war ended in Europe that spring, things did not grow easier for me. Grant came back only four times, and despite his best efforts, he could not manage to charm my folks. They were the only people who seemed totally immune to his appeal, which I put down to the fact that they were stubborn as mules. But I managed to while away the summer, living for the times that Grant came to Philadelphia, pestering him constantly to set a date. He could see how hard it was for me at home, and I was growing desperate to get out and get married.

But Grant would not be pinned down. This only made me even more frantic. We quarreled a lot that summer, which was especially hard for Grant. He hated arguments. He loved the good times, loved to laugh, loved to be with friends and dance the night away. When I kept pressuring him about the wedding, and then got angry when he would not commit a date, his mouth turned down at the edges. His forehead scrunched into furrows, and he tried to hide his thoughts by refusing to look at me. Before my eyes, he turned into a little boy. A spoiled one.

Then in August victory was declared against Japan. Grant came home again three weeks later. He was very excited. He said he had a chance to start an airfreight company with a couple of army buddies. They would be based in the countryside north of London, and fly all over Europe. But it meant that he would not be coming back to live in America.

Oh, perhaps I knew it even then. Perhaps that was why I insisted, and refused to hear his objections. But by that time I had been living in an impossible situation at home for almost a year. I couldn't tell my folks that they had been right all along, and I had been wrong. I couldn't. So I calmly told Grant that it was no problem, I would come and live with him in England. I would simply move to that little village where he had been staying.

Grant tried his best to dissuade me. He did everything but break off the engagement. Which, of course, was what he wanted to do. But Grant was not the kind of man to face up to adversity. His way of dealing with problems was to hop in a plane and fly away from them.

He said yes to all my plans, his mouth forming the word while his eyes said no. But I heard what I wanted to hear. Of course, I later realized he hoped all along that I would not find a way over.

I did not tell my family a thing, but I had to tell my workmates, after swearing them to secrecy. I could not afford a plane ticket—back then, three Atlantic crossings by air cost as much as a new house. And there were no passenger ships operating that close to the war's end. Even the *Queen Elizabeth* and the *Queen Mary*, the finest passenger ships ever built, had been turned into troop carriers. But because my company was big in the shipping business, and because of all our military connections, my boss searched and finally found me a berth. I waited until the day before my departure to send Grant a telegram, telling him that I was coming.

My friends at work threw a big bash for me. I had let them all believe that Grant was begging me to come, and the plans for our wedding were set. The lies I had told stuck in my throat, and my smile felt frozen to my face as I accepted their envy and best wishes and hugs. I spent the entire party gazing around the room, asking myself if I would ever see any of these people again, and wondering what on earth I had gotten myself into.

The night before I was to leave, I told my sister. We had a good old cry together. Then I wrote my parents a note. That took almost five hours. I kept crumpling up the sheets and starting over. I did not want to let any trace of my bitterness seep through. Goodness only knew when I would see them again.

THE TRANSOM CAB that took me across London was high and boxy and had two cracked windows and no heat. The driver sat out front, his seat open to the weather. He was bundled up in a greatcoat and scarf, with a battered cap pulled down over his ears. His hands were chapped as red as burning coals, and he smoked a cigarette the entire trip, puffing and snorting and hawking without ever taking the thing from his lips.

My first view of London frightened me. I felt a little light-headed in any case. My cough was not as persistent, but I could feel the flush of fever. It only made what I was seeing beyond my dirty cracked window seem even more unreal.

I thought I knew what it meant to live through the war years. Back home in America, more families than I cared to count had flown little flags from their front porches, signaling to the world that they had lost a loved one in Europe or Africa or Asia. But in that short journey across London, I learned that America had been spared more than I had ever dreamed possible.

Destruction was everywhere. One building would be completely intact, and the next would be nothing but a pile of rubble. Men and women still worked in the flat metal helmets I had seen in the Movietone News, and several times I saw real bombs that had been dug from the wreckage.

The city seemed too spent to reform itself fully for the new day. Clouds hung down heavy like a sunlit shroud. Distant buildings were gray silhouettes cut from the shadows of the past five years. Church spires rose in the mist like cardboard cutouts. The River Thames was a silent gray mirror, revealing nothing about this enigmatic land.

I had no trouble buying my ticket at Paddington, which

was good, because I was beginning to feel much worse. I showed the agent the card with Grant's address, accepted the ticket, and gave him a large bill. I asked for the platform and scooped up my change. I searched, but could not find a porter. My cases were beginning to feel very heavy.

The crowded station was far too quiet. I realized the city had seemed the same way, but it was only here in the station's enclosed space that I recognized how subdued everyone was. And pale. The faces around me looked as if they had not seen the sun in years. Even the children had dark circles under their eyes. The station held the atmosphere of a giant funeral procession, people silenced by a shared sorrow. Or so it seemed to me.

By the time I reached my platform I was feeling so sweaty and weak that my thoughts flitted in and out of my head. I was definitely running a fever. Down at the far end, where the great curved steel-and-glass station opened to the elements, a heavy snow began to fall.

When we arrived at Reading, where I had to change for the local train to Arden, I was feeling very ill. Thankfully, I did not have to wait long for my train. I collapsed into my seat, and immediately fell into a very troubled sleep. I was perspiring heavily, but I did not have the strength to take off my coat.

I would have missed Arden entirely, except for the fact that the train ended there. I started to wakefulness when the conductor came through, clanging doors and shouting for all to change here. My suitcases weighed a ton. I dragged them and myself off to the platform. It was snowing so hard I could scarcely see the little brick station building. I craned and searched, and began calling Grant's name. He had to be there. I had come all this way for him, and I needed him desperately.

"Is everything all right, Miss?"

The conductor's face swam in front of me. He had a gray walrus moustache and very concerned eyes. I mumbled, "My fiancé . . . he was supposed, supposed to be here."

"You look all done in, Miss. Here, come inside the station for a tick." He picked up my cases. "You say someone was to meet you?"

"Yes, Grant, he's my fiancé. He was, he promised, he asked me to marry . . ."

"Miss? Are you all right?"

I opened my mouth to say I wanted to see Grant, but my legs chose that moment to give way. I would have dropped to the snow-covered concrete, except the conductor moved swiftly to catch me. The last thing I knew, he was shouting for someone to get out right smart and give him a hand.

SIX

The next few days passed in a blur. Waking and sleeping melted together. I dreamed that Grant had come to rescue me, and then he disappeared, and when I woke up and wanted to go look for him, hands pressed me back into the bed. I cried his name and wept, because I was afraid if I didn't go after him, he would be gone forever.

I awoke one morning, and knew the worst was over. I was so weak I could not sit up without help. My cough sounded like a cement truck. But I could feel that the fever had finally eased. I looked around me, seeing things clearly for the very first time. I was in a long room with maybe a dozen beds, all of them full. My bed was hard and the sheets stiff with starch, and the room smelled of disinfectant and medicine. At the room's far end, a tiny Christmas tree stood on a table draped with a sheet. I stared at it for the longest time, and knew two things with utter certainty. How I knew was not important. There was simply no room for questioning. I had missed Christmas, and Grant was gone.

"You're awake then, are you? Excellent." A matron in a uniform so stiff it rustled as she walked came over to stand beside my bed. "You were beginning to worry us."

Her no-nonsense manner helped me to focus. "Where am I?"

"Arden Clinic. The women's ward."

"What day is it?"

"The twenty-seventh of December. You've been here for five days." She inserted a thermometer into my mouth, grasped my wrist in strong fingers, lifted the watch pinned to her lapel, and took my pulse. She inspected the thermometer, made a notation in the metal file by my bed, and announced, "We've finally managed to get your temperature down. Doctor will be pleased. Now you've just enough time to have a bite of breakfast before Doctor makes his rounds."

"I'm not hungry." Hearing the date made me certain the other fact was also true. Grant was gone. A tear trickled down my face. It was all the crying I had the strength for.

"Don't be silly." She took my refusal to eat as a personal affront. "You've hardly had a bite for days."

She waved an orderly over, and together they lifted me up to a sitting position. She sent him for a tray, and rolled a little table in front of me. "Now I expect you to eat everything, do you hear me?"

I did as I was told, though I didn't taste a thing. I had scarcely finished when the doctor arrived. He was a young man, but he had the face of one who had seen far too much suffering, and his hair was already changing from gray to white. He listened to my chest, had me cough a few times, then settled the stethoscope around his neck. "Your name is Emily Robbins, is that correct?"

"Yes."

"We had to go through your personal effects, I'm afraid. Couldn't be helped. We noticed from your passport that you've just arrived here in this country. We found a card with the name Grant Rockwell and an address here in Arden."

I started to say that he was my fiancé, but something stopped me. Instead, another tear escaped to trickle down my cheek.

My show of emotion made the doctor uncomfortable. He cleared his throat, inspected the chart in his lap, and said, "We've had the police stop by that address several times. No one was home, I'm afraid. Were you expected?"

I decided it would be best to shake my head. But I could not stop another tear from sliding down my cheek.

Again the doctor cleared his throat. "You've been suffering from pneumonia. We've given you rather a large dose of penicillin intravenously, and seem to have brought it under control. But you are still quite weak, and will need to be kept here and observed for a few days more. In the meantime, is there anyone we can contact to inform them where you are?"

I whispered, "No."

He gave me an odd look. "Surely someone must be wondering where you were over Christmas. If you'll just—"

"No. There isn't anyone."

"Well." Exasperated, the doctor rose to his feet. "I don't have time to bother with this. If you change your mind, feel free to speak with the Sister."

I spent the rest of that day and the next dozing, waking to eat and take little halting trips down the ward. The women in the other beds watched my progress in silence, but I could hear them whispering when I had passed. I was the mystery woman, an American who had just dropped off the boat and landed in this village clinic.

Visiting hours were the worst. For three hours each afternoon the ward was filled with strangers. After they had stopped by the beds, they would peer openly at me. I had become the ward's favorite topic of conversation.

Two days later, I was awakened from a light doze by the sound of footsteps stopping by my bed. "Miss Robbins?"

I opened my eyes to inspect a very tired young man in a dark suit and a clerical collar. He tried for a smile, but only managed to stretch the pallid skin of his face. "My name is Colin Albright. I'm sorry to wake you, but I only have a moment. Do you mind if I sit down?"

"I guess not." But I was not altogether sure I wanted to be visited by someone who had so little time for me that he had to wake me up.

"Thank you. I'm the assistant vicar at the local parish church. The police stopped by yesterday, and explained that you were here and refused to tell them, that is, you didn't seem to have any contact within the village."

"That's right." Rising irritation gave strength to my voice. "I don't."

"I, ah, that is, the police asked me to stop by the address found in your purse. I spoke with the landlady." He pulled an envelope from his pocket. By now the people surrounding the beds to either side were listening openly. "The house was indeed rented to a Mr. Grant Rockwell, the name I believe you had on your card. But he has gone away."

Whatever shred of hope I had was being torn into tatters by this tired young man. "Gone away?"

"Departed from England. For Berlin, according to the landlady, who lives next door, by the way. But the rent has been paid up through the end of next month, and the landlady was told to expect you." His hand dived back into the pocket and extracted a slip of paper. "Here, I've written down her name. And mine, and the church telephone number, in case you would like to have a chat."

As I looked unseeing at the paper in my hand, the young vicar gave his watch a swift glance and stifled a sigh of impatience.

I was flooded with a bitterness so acrid I felt my throat burning. "Thank you, but I wouldn't want to take any more of your precious time. You're so busy already."

He rose from the chair as though it had been spring-loaded. "Right. I'll be off then." He was either too tired or too preoccupied to have room for any irritation of his own. He realized he was still holding the envelope. "Oh, and Mr. Rockwell left this for you. Good day, Miss Robbins."

Ignoring the stares from all about me, I opened the envelope and read the letter. Or tried to. The words swam on the page. But I knew what it said. Grant had avoided this little problem as he did all others, by flying away.

His words were exasperated and sorrowful in turn. I let

my hand and the letter fall to my lap. There was no escaping the truth now. I was in a foreign country, in a strange village, abandoned by the man I had traveled four thousand miles to marry, and utterly alone.

The orderly happened to walk by and notice my state. He unbuttoned the curtain and whipped it around my bed. But nothing could be done to muffle the sound of my sobs.

SEVEN

When Marissa awoke, she glanced at the bedside clock and saw that it was just before midnight. She had a dim recollection of growing very tired over dinner, trying to hide it because she did not want her grandmother to stop talking. But suddenly the fork in her hand had become hard to lift, and her eyelids had felt as though they weighed a ton each. Her grandmother had helped her upstairs and into bed, promising to continue the story when she awoke.

Marissa lay and listened to the house creaking and pinging about her. She loved the way the old place spoke at night, as though reliving the years of footsteps and laughter that had filled the big rooms. Her mother had been born and raised in this house. It gave Marissa a sense of permanence and safety, even in such a troubling time, to know that she slept in a house that had been theirs for so long.

A fool in love. It had been so strange to hear Gran describe herself in that way. And yet the confession had formed an instant bonding between them, one that had grown increasingly strong as the story continued. Even now, lying here in the dark, Marissa could feel the invisible threads of honesty and remembrance drawing their hearts together.

Marissa vividly recalled how Gran's face had changed with the telling. Her features had taken on different lines, as though the act of remembering transported her. Marissa felt as though she had watched her grandmother return to another time, and another place as well. Another time, another place, and in some strange way, another person.

Despite the unsettling tale, Marissa felt the sharing was both good and important. Strange that she would think of something good coming out of this difficult time. But that was exactly how it felt. Without understanding how she knew, Marissa was certain that she was hearing not just a story, but a vital message as well.

As she lay there wondering what the lesson might be, she saw an image of her brother's face. Instantly her whole body burned with shame. And guilt. There was no longer the shield of her anger to hide behind. Somehow hearing her grandmother's tale had wiped away the veil of bitterness over her own plight.

Buddy, her Buddy, was the brother who had always been there for her. As far back as she could remember, Buddy had stood by her, explained things to her, played whatever game she had invented. He even sat through tea parties with her dolls because he loved her and that was just Buddy's way. No matter that he would rather have been out playing football or climbing trees. He was always ready to step in and protect and defend and explain. Buddy with a heart as big as all outdoors, and she had wounded him. And not just him. Memories of what she had said to her family clenched her heart.

Marissa looked at the clock once more, then calculated the difference in time between Philadelphia and Hawaii. It would still be afternoon, she decided. She bit her lip at the thought of what was to come, but knew it could not be put off any longer.

She slipped from her bed and pulled on her robe and slippers. She tiptoed across the floor, the night-light giving her just enough illumination to see her grandmother asleep on the folding bed in the corner. Thankfully the door to the hall was open, because it creaked something awful. Steadying herself with one hand on the stair railing, Marissa walked downstairs.

There were a lot of differences between what had happened to her grandmother, and what she was going through. She hadn't missed this trip through any fault of her own.

But hearing of her grandmother's suffering helped put her own troubles into perspective. It propelled her into the kitchen, and gave her the strength to pick up the phone and dial the number on the paper taped to the wall, and ask the hotel operator for her parents' room.

When the familiar voice came on the phone, her first words were, "I'm sorry, Momma." And suddenly she was trying so hard not to give in to the tears. But she could feel the weeping deep inside her, wanting to come out, making her whole body tremble. "I was awful."

"Oh, darling, darling. You were just being human. I'm just sorry as I can be that you aren't here with us."

She could hear the tears in her mother's voice, and her own could not be kept back another instant. "I'm sorry.

Really. I wish I could take back everything I said."

"It's all forgotten and forgiven. I miss you so, my little princess."

"I miss you too." They spoke for a few moments more, neither of them paying as much attention to what was said as to the fact that they were speaking. Then she asked, "Is Buddy there?"

"Yes, hold on." Carol sniffed loudly, and set the phone down.

Marissa listened to her mother coax Buddy to talk with her. And that hurt worse than anything. "It's all right, honey," she heard her mother say. "She's fine. Really. And she wants to speak with you."

There was a long pause, and then a very sad voice said softly, "Hello."

Marissa felt as though she was breaking apart inside. She had hurt her Buddy so much he didn't want to speak to her. She sobbed so hard she couldn't say anything at all.

And then she heard that he was crying, too, just bawling away on the other end of the phone. And she managed to whine out around the sobs, "Oh, Buddy, I'm so sorry."

He caught his breath with a hiccup, and whispered, "It's okay."

"No, it's not. I wouldn't hurt you for anything. Not ever."

"Mom told us it was the sickness."

"That's right. Wait a minute, okay?" She put down the phone, went over to the sink, and tore off a paper towel. She wiped her eyes, blew her nose, took a deep breath, another, and forced herself to steady. Then she picked up the phone and said, "I want you to do something for me. I want you to go out and have a great time."

Hearing she was back in control gave him the strength to breathe hard, and say, "Okay."

"I mean it. You have to have a double good time, one for you and one for me. You have to do *everything*. Do you hear me? The only way I'll know anything about it is from what you tell me."

"Dad gave me a camera for Christmas. He said I needed to take pictures for you."

"Lots and lots of them." She wiped away the tears that continued to spill over. "And remember everything you see, okay? Because when you come home you have to tell me."

"Okay, Sis. I'll try."

"I love you, Buddy."

"I love you, too. I wish you were here. It's not the same. Nothing is."

"I know. Put Momma back on, okay?"

In just a few seconds Carol was asking, "How are you feeling?"

"Tired. But Gran is taking good care of me."

"I'm sure she is. You're here with us, honey. We hold you close in our hearts."

"I love you, too, Mom. And I'm so sorry."

"There's nothing to be sorry for. It's all behind us, all right? You just stay busy getting well."

Marissa waited until the tears had stopped before going back upstairs. Gran was in the same position she had been in when Marissa left. But as she climbed back into bed, she heard a quiet voice say, "I'm very proud of you, honey. You did the right thing."

"I was just awful," she said, then bit down hard, because she didn't want the tears to start back.

"Well, it's okay now." Gran rolled over in her little bed. "Are you sleepy?"

"No, not really. I'm sorry, I didn't mean to wake you up."

"It doesn't matter. Old folks don't need sleep like young people do. Would you like some hot chocolate?"

Suddenly that sounded like the best thing in the whole world. "Oh yes. And would you tell me what happened next?"

"Of course I will." Gran rose to her feet, turned on the lamp, and smiled at Marissa across the room. "I'll be right back."

GRAN'S STORY

On the last day of the year, they finally let me out of the clinic. I felt much better by then, and had been asking them to release me for several days. But they refused, supposedly because I had nobody to look after me if the fever returned. I think it was also partly because they wanted to punish me for refusing to answer their questions.

I felt eyes follow me out of the ward, down the hall, and into the front lobby. They had called for the village's only taxi to come and take me, because I was still too weak to carry my bags very far, and because I didn't know where Grant's house was. None of the nurses or the doctor had much to say to me while I waited. I signed the papers and sat on the hard wooden bench, my cases at my feet, and knew that they were irritated with how I had refused to feed their curiosity.

The taxi driver finally came in, a gnarled and knobby little man who doffed his cap and proudly displayed his remaining four teeth. "Down to Wharfe Lane, are you, Miss?"

"I think so, yes." Grateful to be leaving the stares and the whispers behind, I followed him outside. After being cooped up inside for so long, the snow-covered lane and the crisp winter air and the billowing storm clouds overhead seemed strangely invigorating. Then I glanced in the direction we were headed, and I stopped to stare at his vehicle.

"Never seen a gas bag, then." He wheezed a chuckle as he heaved the cases into the front compartment. "Ain't too many of them still about, but this one's served me well. My engine's been set to burn a lot of gas and just a little petrol. With that bag there, I can go almost a week on one tank. Petrol is easier to come by these days, but long as the rationing's still on, I'll keep her for safety's sake."

The boxy little car was dwarfed by a great metal cage attached to its roof and sliding over its rear end. In this cage was stuffed a bulging black balloon. The cold wind buffeted the apparatus, causing the entire cab to shake and roll.

He saw me into the backseat, offered me a thick horse blanket, then settled in front. "You'll like it down there, you will. Good sort, those folk. Like to know everybody's business, but that's village life for you."

Just what I needed, I thought to myself, more curiosity hounds. As soon as he started off, I understood what the blanket was for. The car had heat, but it also had holes in the floorboards. My upper body was surrounded by the heater's oily fumes, but my feet and legs were freezing. Swiftly I wrapped the blanket around my legs, and planted one end under my shoes. "Is it very far?"

"A fair piece, much as you can have and stay in the village. Wharfe Lane sits right down by the river's edge." He rattled on down the hill, and gave someone on the sidewalk a cheery wave. "Dropped a customer off this morning, had a chat with your landlady. She's a right one, old Rachel Ballard. Can't wait to be making your acquaintance."

"I'll bet." I could just see her, fat and round as a butter ball, with a huge nose that she loved to stick into other people's business. There was no telling what Grant had told her.

Then a thought struck me with a force that made my cheeks flame. What if I wasn't the first lost and forlorn little thing to show up at Grant's doorstep? What if the whole village was laughing behind their hands? Oh, look, there goes another of Grant's floozies, and this one all the way from America, can you imagine. I flipped the collar up on my coat, and buried my face out of view. Yes, I could just bet the landlady was looking forward to meeting me.

The taxi took a sudden turn, and there at the bottom of the road was water. A large flowing stretch of it. "What is that?"

"That?" My question caused the driver to laugh out loud.

"Why, that's the River Thames, Miss. Didn't you know we're a river village?"

"I suppose I did." Of course. The town's name was Arden-on-Thames. But I had no idea the river was so close.

The road seemed to simply drop into the water. As we drew closer, I saw how it took a right-hand bend and went up to join with an old stone bridge.

But the taxi did not follow the road around. Instead, it took a sharp turn to the left, down a tiny cobblestone lane. The alley was so narrow that no one could pass the taxi when its doors were opened.

The driver pulled up and stopped. "Here we are, Miss."

Hesitantly, I inspected my new home through the grimy window of the taxi. There was not much to see. The entire street was one long wall of two-story houses all joined together. They looked like the neatly painted brick tenements of a big city. But this was a small village, and tenements had no place here.

"Fred, yoo-hoo, I say, Fred!"

"There's your landlady now," the driver said, opening his door. He scrambled from the taxi and doffed his cap. "Fine morning, Miss Rachel."

"Oh, it's not, it's cold and it's dreadful and you still haven't done a thing about that horrid floor of yours, have you?" The woman coming their way was limping heavily and leaning upon a cane. She stopped and huffed a moment, then finished, "Shame on you, Fred."

The driver responded with another grin. "I put the blanket in like you said, Miss Rachel."

"That's not good enough. It simply won't do." She started toward my side of the taxi. "To think our new arrival has been forced to rattle about our little town in such a condition!"

I opened my door and rose to greet her. Only then did I realize how tall the woman was. She had to be over six feet in height. She was stooped somewhat, and she walked with difficulty, but still she had a regal bearing. And a grand light to her eyes.

"Oh, my *dear*," she said. "If only I could have come up and gathered you myself. But the old banger caught a terrific cold last year and I still haven't managed to obtain the required parts." She frowned at Fred, as though it was all his fault. "A dreadful state, if you ask me."

I was caught flatfooted. The only thing I could think to say was my name. "I'm Emily Robbins."

"Well, of course you are. And I should have been up to see you long before now. But I came down with the worst influenza, which of course was the last thing you needed breathed upon you. All sorts of germs are floating about these days. It's the cold, you know, they're predicting the worst winter since the last war."

She gave her head an impatient shake. "Then when I was better, that new doctor we've been saddled with actually ordered me to stay well away from the clinic."

She snorted her derision, which instantly warmed me to her. I didn't like the doctor either.

Rachel went on, "I told him time and time again, the young lady needs a bit of company, especially over the

Christmas holidays. But he kept going on about the new babies and such. He actually claimed he would bar the doors if I came up! Can you imagine such nonsense?"

I decided I liked this tall, angular woman. Enough, in fact, to confess, "I was very lonely."

The words brought a great ballooning of her emotional sails. "Well, of *course* you were." She hefted her cane and shook it fiercely. "I didn't half give him a piece of my mind, I can tell you that. But you see how much good it did. Nobody pays any attention to an old woman. Not these days."

"There's a chill wind blowing down the lane, Miss Rachel," the driver pointed out.

"Quite right, Fred. Come along, my dear. We mustn't be keeping you out here in your condition." She reached into the pocket of her shapeless sweater-coat and came up with a bundle of keys. A skeleton key almost four inches long was used to unlock the red door. "I came by this morning to light the heater and dust a bit. Couldn't manage more than that, I'm afraid. I'm only a few days out of bed myself, and all the energy I have has been spent up at the College. There's far too much that's gone undone while I've been lying abed, don't you know. Poor Colin can only see to so much on his own, and most of the others wouldn't know to wipe their own noses unless someone's there to tell them how."

I did not understand what she was talking about, but decided it did not matter. Her voice was the nicest thing I had heard since stepping off the boat. I followed Rachel into a very small, very plain front room. It was not much warmer than outside. A disused fireplace stood empty and cold in one corner. Three high-backed chairs and a cracked side table were the room's only furnishings. I said doubtfully, "You didn't have to go to any trouble on my account."

"Nonsense, of course I did." She flicked on the light switch, illuminating a single bulb in a white ceiling fixture. The room still looked faded and full of cold shadows. "Now I want you to give Fred here some money. Fred, go down to the shops and buy her some provisions." Her long age-spotted hands dived back into her pocket. "Here, I've made you out a list."

"The rationing's still on, Miss Rachel."

"Oh, stuff and nonsense. She has to eat, hasn't she? And how on earth is she supposed to have a ration card when she's been laid out in the clinic since she arrived?"

Fred mulled that one over, then brightened. "I'll have the grocer put it on Mr. Grant's card."

The saying of his name was like a knife stabbing straight to my heart. Rachel shot me a swift knowing glance, then said, "Of course you will. I should have thought of that myself. Tell Bob I'll drop the card by myself later on."

"Right you are, Miss Rachel." The driver accepted my bill with another doffing of his cap. "I'll bring your cases up with the provisions, Miss. Don't you worry now, Miss Rachel will see you right, sure enough."

The kind words and the unspoken knowledge behind them brought a burning to my eyes. Rachel's shrewd gaze caught that as well, for she turned me around and guided me to the stairwell. "Up here, my dear. Let me show you your new home."

Home. Despite my best efforts to maintain control, sorrow was an overpowering vacuum that drew me in. So many dreams had been contained in that one word, *home.*

I followed her up the stairs and down a narrow hallway. Upstairs, the house was warm and cozy. As we entered the front parlor, I swallowed the lump in my throat, and said, "It's very nice."

And it was. The room was small but very tastefully appointed, with mahogany double doors and a matching built-in cupboard. The fireplace was black marble, with a mahogany mantel. The furniture was old and worn, but welcoming. Big windows and another mahogany door, this one with a glass centerpiece, looked out over a nice little balcony. Beyond the balcony flowed the river.

There was no sign of Grant having ever been there. None at all. Suddenly I understood what Rachel had meant by a bit of dusting.

"The structure itself is Victorian, designed and built around 1890. It was turned into a series of row houses about thirty years ago." Rachel stood in the center of the little parlor and surveyed it with a critical eye. "It's all rather in need of a dash of paint and a bit of work, I'm afraid."

"It's wonderful. Really." I stepped to the window and looked out over the river. It flowed gray and silent beneath the blustering storm. The banks on the other side lay still and white. Hills rose into the lowering clouds, disappearing like quiet old men gathered beneath a floating veil. A sigh escaped from my heart. It would have made a lovely home.

"Yes, the view is what makes this place so special."

Rachel moved up beside me. Her natural effervescence was quietened. She looked out over the river and said confidentially, "We bought this place for our boy, Samuel. We lost him over Normandy."

I turned from the river. "I'm so sorry."

"The one good thing about it all, if I can call it that, was that my husband passed on the year the war began. Otherwise the loss of Samuel would have killed him stone dead, and I couldn't have managed the two losses at once." The lines on her face deepened, her tone dropped. "He was our only child, you see, and we had him rather late in life. A grand boy. A flier. Just like your Grant."

She cast me a quick little smile, one at direct odds to the hollow grieving in her gaze. "That's why we decided to let this flat to him, you see. Grant was so much like our boy. Tall and dashing and devil-may-care."

"A laugh for every problem, a smile for every girl," I said, and could not keep the quiver from my voice.

"Oh, you mustn't think Grant did not care for you, my dear." Rachel turned her gaze toward the river, allowing me privacy in this intimate moment. "He spoke of you as he spoke of none other."

"But he's gone," I said, wiping my eyes.

"Yes, well, some men are not the marrying kind. They are meant to soar the heavens in search of adventure and glory." Rachel took a ragged breath and drew herself up taller. "That is what has kept me going, you see. Thinking that perhaps my Samuel was never truly meant for this earth, not in the way of most mortals. He came and splashed us all with the light of heaven, did his part for God and country, and left us richer for having known him. Even for a little while. Even when the loss is a wound that shall never heal."

Rachel turned away from both the window and me, raising up one corner of her sweater to wipe at her eyes. She hobbled across to the doors, and said with forced cheerfulness, "I'll leave you to rest a bit and get settled. Fred can set your cases and the provisions by the stairs." She stopped in the doorway, and said without turning around, "I must ask a favor of you. If you're up to it, could you perhaps accompany me to church for the New Year's service this evening?"

I was about to tell her that I couldn't. I was too tired, too weak, too anything so long as it kept me from having to face a church full of curious eyes. But something held me back. I felt as though a strong yet gentle hand had settled over my mouth.

"There will be words of remembrance, you see," Rachel went on, her back still to me and the room. "I find such outings hard going on my own, don't you know. So many of my friends will be locked in their own grief. Most of us have lost someone close. I don't see how I could possibly burden them with my own woes just now, but I am not sure I can hear those words alone."

"Of course I'll come," I said weakly, not understanding at all what was tugging at my heart.

Rachel released a sigh, one that sounded as though she had been holding it ever since we met. "That is so very kind of you, my dear. You have a nice rest, and I'll be back for you around eight."

EIGHT

I ate and rested and ate again, aching with the emptiness of moving about what should have been our house, sleeping in what could have been my marriage bed. Then in the afternoon I felt strong enough to do something that could not wait. I bundled myself in layer after layer and went out.

It was hard to believe this was truly New Year's Eve. Other than a fly-specked banner in the grocer's window, no doubt left over from years gone by, there was little to suggest this day was different from any other. People moved down the snow-covered walks in cautious haste, so hidden beneath layers of old dark-colored clothes I could scarcely make out whether they were male or female. There was little conversation, and none of the festivities that must have been going on back home. Only once did I hear someone wish another a Happy New Year.

Yet despite my best efforts to convince myself otherwise, the village of Arden-on-Thames held a truly charming air. The softly falling snow and empty streets helped transport it back to an earlier era. The frills and laces of a red-brick Victorian gothic structure stood alongside a staid Queen Anne cottage and that beside a bowed Elizabethan building, one that dated from before the American colonies were settled. I was so very glad to be out of the clinic and strong enough to be walking around. The freedom meant a great deal, and the air was crisp and cold and held a clean snowy taste I loved.

I arrived at my destination, very pleased that I had found my way back. A shop I had passed in the taxi had displayed a P & O Steamship placard in the window. I inspected the snow-dashed display, and saw that this was indeed a travel agent. But the cruise poster was so old that the women's dresses had gone out of style and were back in fashion again.

Inside the shop had a dismal, disused air. One elderly woman sat behind a long counter, and seemed utterly astounded that I had decided to enter. "Can I help you?"

"I'd like a ticket to America. A steamer." I selected one of a half-dozen chairs lining my side of the counter. All of them bore a layer of dust.

The woman brightened immensely. "Ah, you must be the American lady. I heard they let you out of the clinic today."

I felt my cheeks grow bright red, but I was determined not to be put off. "As soon as possible, please."

"I'm afraid that won't be easy, my dear. All passages to and from the British Isles are restricted to a 'need-only' basis." She gave me a cheery smile. "Which is their way of saying that we need not apply, as we'd only be wasting our time."

I was in no mood for polite jokes. "But there must be something."

"There isn't, I'm afraid. You only need read the papers to understand." Clearly she was delighted with the company, and in no hurry to send me on my way. "Over thirty thousand children were sent to Canada and America when the Jerries started bombing our cities. The families are clamoring for them to come home."

"But I'm going the other way."

"Even worse, I'm afraid. There've been protests in Washington, I saw it on the Movietone News just the other day. Went to see the new Fred Astaire and Ginger Rogers movie. I say, can all American gents dance like him?"

"Not all." I leaned back. I, too, had heard about the protests. Mothers from all over America had gathered in Washington, carrying signs and shouting for the government to "Bring Our Boys Home." "So all the berths are going to troops?"

"Afraid so. Unless you've got some connection, there's almost nothing I can do."

Which left me with just one choice, one that I dreaded. "But you will try."

"Well, if you insist, naturally, but there's really—"

I rose before she could finish her protest. "I'll check back next week, hopefully by then you'll have some good news for me."

I closed the door on her halfhearted wishes for the new year, and made my way back home. *Home.* It was a strange word to use for a place that mocked me with its emptiness. I had been such a fool.

After another rest, I awoke to falling dusk. I turned on

the lights around the house, trying to dispel the forlorn shadows. But they seemed to follow me as I went into the kitchen and made dinner. They made unwelcome company throughout the evening, so that when Rachel came by to collect me for church, I was down the stairs in a flash.

"You can't possibly imagine what it means to have you come along, my dear," she said, carefully making her way over the snow-covered cobblestones. "I am in your debt."

Those were not exactly the words I would have expected to hear from my landlady. It seemed as good a time as any to relate my troubles. "I went by the travel agent to see about a ticket home."

"Yes, Mabel told me." At the end of the lane, she used her cane to point us across the main road and into a narrow path between two aged buildings. "Through there, my dear."

"Mabel is the travel agent?"

"A rather glorious title for someone who sits there day in and day out only because she has no one to go home to, wouldn't you say?" The lane opened into the church graveyard. "Her husband is retired navy, and they put him to work overseeing something down at the Portsmouth docks. Both her boys are in Singapore awaiting berths home. But at least they survived."

The churchyard was wrapped in a stillness that seemed utterly beyond time and worldly care. Most of the snow-capped gravestones were so ancient their engravings had long since washed away. Ringing the tiny yard were almshouses, low stone homes given by the church to needy parishioners. A placard in the wall we passed declared they had been built in 1510 and renovated four hundred years later.

Rachel went on, "There are a lot of such people about these days, I'm afraid. I read recently that less than a fifth of our boys have been brought home from the fronts. There isn't transport, you see, nor enough resources to fit them out for civvy street. And that's speaking of just the lucky ones, of course."

The gaslights fronting the church illuminated quiet clusters of people. I slowed, held by the image of faces turning our way. "Does everybody know about me and my troubles?"

Rachel halted and leaned heavily on her cane. She faced me, so I could see her smile. "Oh, I would imagine there is a poor bedridden soul somewhere in the village, one with failing eyesight and worse hearing, who has not been kept abreast of your arrival."

"Great," I muttered. "Just great."

"There's no getting around it, I'm afraid. At present you are Arden-on-Thames's favorite mystery." The smile broadened. "Just having you under my roof has elevated my social status considerably."

"Glad I could be of assistance to someone," I said, turning back toward the empty house.

"Oh, you mustn't leave me now, my dear. Please." Rachel grasped my arm with desperate fingers. "I would be placed at the mercy of the Grim Brigade."

"The what?"

"That's my name for them, of course." She gave me a tug and a pleading look. "Come along, I'll show you what I mean."

Despairing over the prospect of being stared at for hours by the entire village, I allowed Rachel to pull me forward.

Gray shadows took on form and substance, becoming a steady stream of people walking toward the church entrance. It was a grand old structure, built of stones five feet across, with a square Norman tower and scarred oak doors a full thirty feet high.

Rachel released my arm to point at a cluster of women standing by the doors. "Now Claire, she's a neighbor of ours. She lost her son to Rommel in Africa. And Fiona, she's the short dumpy one, all three of her daughters have run off with American airmen. Can't say I blame them. Her husband is too busy propping up the corner of his favorite pub to have noticed their going."

We emerged from the shadows. I steeled myself at the fear of having all faces turned toward me. But it did not happen. There were a few glances, yes, and perhaps some recognition and whispers. But most people seemed lost in their own thoughts and quiet conversations. There was none of the cheer I would have expected for a New Year's service, especially one coming at the end of a long, hard war. All was quiet and somber.

"Christine, now, there's a sad case for you. Three sons lost in the space of three months, and her husband by a heart attack two weeks after they buried the last one."

"That's awful," I murmured.

"It is indeed." Rachel drew herself up until she was almost a full head taller than I, and gave the group a solemn, "Good evening, ladies."

A scattering of murmurs came our way, no real words I could hear. But their expressions seared my heart. Such bitterness, such pinched hardness, such scathing gazes. I was very glad when Rachel did not stop, but rather led me through the doors and into the church. Once inside, she continued in a whisper, "Ever since Samuel's plane went down, they've been trying to claim me. Hmph. As though I were now theirs by right."

She guided me into a pew, nodded to our neighbors, then thumped her cane on the ancient slate floor as she said, "I will not give in to the temptations of bitterness and hatred. I will not indulge myself in useless anger. I will not."

I heard almost nothing of the service. I stood and sat with the others, following Rachel's lead. I stared at the prayer book and the hymnal, but I could not make out the words. My thoughts remained locked upon what Rachel had said as we seated ourselves. *The temptations of bitterness and hatred and useless anger.* They loomed before me like towering idols, lures to draw me into a darkness I had not even noticed.

The candlelit church became a huge stone mirror. I had blamed the shadows filling the empty house on Grant, when in truth they were there in my own heart. I sat in the ancient church and felt the stains of my own mistakes, filling my forlorn heart, whispering their vulture cries, seeking to draw me in and away.

It would be so easy to give in, I knew that with utter certainty. I had every reason to follow the lead of those ladies outside the church. And if I did, in time my own face would come to look like theirs, pinched and bitter and defeated by my own acrid spirit.

It was only with difficulty that I rose and followed Rachel down the aisle at the service's close. The night and the surroundings did not come back into focus until I recognized the robed man standing at the church doors. It was the assistant vicar, the one who had delivered Grant's letter. He looked dignified and wise beyond his years, standing there in his flowing robes, greeting each person in turn.

When it came my turn to stand before him, he gave me a little bow, "Miss Robbins, do I have that correct?"

Suddenly the anger I had felt in the clinic was there with me again. Despite all that I had just realized about myself, I could not keep the acid from my voice. "Amazing that a man as busy as you can remember something so unimportant."

My words drove him a half-step back. In doing so, he moved beneath the nave's single light. It illuminated the finely drawn cast to his features, the deep circles under his eyes. He did not look tired. He looked exhausted.

Reverend Albright recovered and gave me a stiff little nod. "I am glad to see you up and about," he murmured. "Thank you for joining us." Then he turned to the next person in line.

Rachel waited until we were picking our way down the churchyard path. "I say, you were rather rough on young Colin back there, weren't you?"

Bitterly I recounted how the only person who had visited me in the hospital had been too busy to do more than drop off Grant's letter, and had never returned. But Rachel did not respond with the sympathy I expected. At least, not to me. Instead, when I finished she said thoughtfully, "Colin is less at fault than you might think."

"I don't see how."

"No, of course not." The lane was transformed by the snow and the night into a fairyland of houses sleeping beyond the reach of time or woes. "It occurs to me, my dear, that you might like to join me tomorrow for a little excursion."

"Thanks, Rachel, but I've got an excursion of my own to make."

"Well, never mind. If you change your mind, though, I'm up there most mornings."

"Up where?"

"Ah, that would be telling." Rachel stopped in front of her house and graced me with another of her smiles. "Thank you so much for accompanying me this evening, my dear."

"It was nice," I replied. "Happy New Year, Rachel."

"And to you the same, my dear. To you the same." Her eyes held a keen note, a searching reminder of all I had faced within the church. "May you be blessed with eternal riches and God's infinite peace." She gave me a quick one-arm hug. "That was what my dear mum used to say to us each year. Never have I felt the need for her blessing more than now."

"I know what you mean," I said, and turned away so she could not see the sudden rush of tears. "Good night."

Once upstairs, I searched through my cases until I found my writing pad and a pen. I took them into the kitchen, which was the house's central room. It had no windows, as these row houses were long and narrow, fronting the river on one end and the lane on the other. There was a skylight, and I could hear the snow flick delicately upon the glass. I felt comforted, being enclosed by the house and the walls. I was as far from the threatening night as I could be. I sat at the little kitchen table, and began to write the two most difficult letters of my entire life.

The first one was to my parents. I had to stop often, because the lines would blur and I needed to see what I was saying. I felt it important to accept fully what I knew now was the truth. I wrote that they had been right all along, that Grant was everything they had thought he was. I asked their forgiveness for all the pain I had caused. I had no excuse for my actions, I said, except for the fact that I had been head over heels in love.

The second letter was to my former boss at the shipping company. I was brutal in my honesty. I felt I was writing the letter as much to myself as to him and everyone else who would sooner or later hear the news. I said I had been abandoned. I was trapped in a little English village, where I knew no one. And I could not book a passage to America.

I begged him for help in finding a berth, and I asked for a job. I explained that I had not wanted to send a telegram, because my parents needed to hear the news from me first. But I was desperate to get out of England, and pleaded with him to help me find a way home.

By the time I finished the second letter, it was after two in the morning. I felt drained and weak. But that was not altogether bad. Hopefully I would be able to sleep and not dream. I was not looking forward to my first night alone in this house.

Wearily I prepared for bed. As I pulled the covers up and over me, I reflected that this was the worst year of my life. And it was only two hours old.

NINE

Marissa had never felt like this before. Never imagined an awakening could be so strange. As she lay there, it seemed as though the dark was coming to take her away. It was a struggle to find the breath just to say, "Gran?"

The shadow in the foldaway bed rolled over. A sleepy voice said, "Honey?"

"Gran, I'm scared."

She rose from the bed, turned on the lamp, slipped on her bedroom slippers, and padded over. "What is it, child?"

"I don't know." Icy fingers seemed to be reaching through her skin, tracing their way up inside her limbs. "Am I dying?"

"No." Gran was fully awake now. "No, you're going to make it through this just fine. Do you hurt?"

"Not exactly. I can't move."

"I'm right here beside you. Do you feel my hand?"

"Yes. It's never been this bad before."

"The illness has to run its course. From this point onward, you'll probably begin to feel better."

But Marissa did not feel as though she would ever recover. Her invisible chains were so strong she could not fight against them. She did not need to sleep, which made it worse in a way. Now the fatigue spilled over from her sleepy times to conquer the moments when she was awake as well. "How do you know so much about this?"

"Ah." Gran's face looked as though she was glad for a reason to smile. "That is part of my story."

"Will you talk to me?"

"You're sure you don't want to sleep, honey?"

"No." Pleading now. "I'm afraid if I slept right now I'd never wake up."

"You mustn't worry about that, sweetheart."

"I'm not sleepy. Really."

"Well." Gran gave her face a light rub. "It seems that our midnight chocolate is going to become a habit."

"You'll have to hold mine. I don't think I can."

"Don't you worry about that for a moment. I'll be right back." As she turned toward the door, she smiled down at her granddaughter and said, "Do you think we deserve an extra marshmallow tonight?"

GRAN'S STORY

The next morning, I knocked on Rachel's door. She opened it so swiftly I stepped back in surprise, only to find she was slipping on her coat and gloves. Her face showed fleeting disappointment when she recognized me, then she gave her already familiar smile. "Oh, good morning, my dear. I thought you were Fred."

"The taxi driver? That's why I came over, I needed to ask him to take me somewhere."

"Come in, come in. There's no telling how long Fred

will be. He was leaving for another job when I rang, and with all this snow the roads must be simply dreadful. Would you care for a tea?"

"That would be nice, thank you." I followed her back inside. "But you're all ready to go."

She set the cane down in the corner by the door, and started up the stairs, leaning heavily upon the railing. "Yes, well, I am impatient to get about my work."

Rachel's house was a mirror image of my own, with a central kitchen and a long hallway connecting to the front room and a balcony overlooking the river. "What work is that?"

"Oh, I'm volunteering up at the War College. Do you know, I believe I'll join you for a cup. How do you take your tea, my dear?"

"A little sugar, please. I'm sorry, where did you say—"

"Oh, just listen to me." Rachel's laugh had a gay ring, and she bustled about the kitchen in an excited manner. "The War College is what it's been called for the past five years, and such names die hard. The Ministry of Defense took over a large manor just outside of town and turned it into an academy for senior officers. They came in for courses on everything from strategy to language to map reading." She poured steaming water into the old teapot. "We had one of these officers stay in your place for a time. Charming fellow. Didn't make it back, I'm afraid. I still talk to his wife from time to time. She came down and joined him while he was here. Took the loss rather hard, poor dear."

I accepted my cup. "It sounds like you can't mention anybody without talking about them losing someone."

"Yes, I suppose it does. There are so many." She sipped at her cup. "Mind you, it hasn't been a bed of roses for those left behind. There are quite a number of grieving ghosts wandering our streets."

I started to ask what she did at the former War College, when the doorbell rang. Her face lit up with renewed excitement. "Oh, that must be Fred!"

I followed her back downstairs, and watched as she flung back the door and said in mock severity. "Shame on you, Fred. I thought for certain you had forgotten me."

Fred doffed his cap and held open the cab door. "Not you, Miss Rachel. Just held up a bit by the snow, is all."

Rachel started to enter, then straightened. "Oh, wait, Emily wanted to ask you something."

I stepped up beside her. "I was wondering if you could take me over to the airfield."

Rachel's face fell. "Oh, my dear. Are you sure that's such a good idea?"

Fred clearly misunderstood, for he said, "Not a hope, Miss Emily. Not today."

To Rachel, I said, "I need to see about a way back to America, and there's no berth available on a ship." To Fred, "Why not?"

"Because the hills are chock full of snow, is why." Fred turned and pointed toward the hills rising behind us. "The airfield's only five miles away, but it's straight up and straight down. All roads over the Chilterns are closed up tight."

I had not thought of that. "What about this afternoon?"

"Not likely. They do all the roads around town first.

Leave it till tomorrow, I say." He glanced up at the heavily laden clouds. "That is, unless we get more snow, which by the look of things could well happen."

"Never mind, my dear." Rachel patted my arm. "You might be better off leaving that for a day or two. And you are welcome to stay here just as long as you like."

"'Course, some of the boys might try to make it in to the local tonight," Fred offered.

"I'm sorry, the what?"

"The local, the pub." Fred was totally oblivious to the dark look Rachel was shooting his way. "The Horse and Groom, just at the top of New Street. The townsfolk call it the Gloom and Doom, don't ask me why. Those Yank flyboys, they claimed it as their own. Take those four-wheel-drive jeeps over roads I wouldn't try in my dreams."

"We should be off, Fred," Rachel said crisply, climbing inside the cab.

But Fred was too busy grinning and talking to pay her any mind. "Had one of 'em tell me they had their nerves surgically removed the day they pinned on their wings. I wouldn't put it past a few of them to try and—"

"Fred!"

"Right away, mum." Fred scampered around to his door.

I stood there, feeling at a loss as to what I should do with my day. Rachel observed my confusion, and leaned back through the door. "My dear, I do wish you would reconsider and join me."

"I'd just be in the way," I replied, though the invitation held the appeal of at least filling the empty hours.

"Oh, piffle." Rachel slid over and patted the seat beside her. "We are so understaffed, I shouldn't be surprised if the day shift didn't fall at your feet in gratitude just for showing up."

"It's the truth, Miss Emily," Fred called from the front seat. "It's a right shambles up there. Why, just the other day they—"

"That is quite enough, Fred," Rachel rapped out. "I am paying you to drive, not spread your dreadful rumors."

"Right you are, Miss Rachel." Fred grinned as he pumped the gas bag lever and pulled on the choke. "Right you are."

THAT MORNING, THE village of Arden appeared straight from a fairy-tale painting. All the ancient buildings stood draped in snow and icicles. The air smelled of wood smoke and winter. Chimneys puffed cheerily, and windows glazed in frost stared back at me. People were made plump by padding, their faces lost behind scarves and hats and shawls.

We climbed the slope leading beyond the clinic and on out of town, up to where the clouds draped lazily over the hills. Forests from a black-and-white etching closed in about us. Little stone cottages appeared now and then, surrounded by snow-covered hedges. In several yards, horses stamped and jingled their harnesses as families loaded carts with crates and milk tins.

"Egg deliveries," Rachel explained. "With the rationing we've returned to earlier times."

"What is it you do at the War College?" I asked.

"Everything under the sun, and then some," Fred offered cheerily.

"That will do, Fred," Rachel said mildly, and patted my knee. "It will be easier to show you than try and describe what has taken place in our little village, my dear."

"Best thing that could have happened, if you ask me," Fred declared.

This time, Rachel did not dispute. Instead, she said to me, "Now as to your trying to find a way back to America, you mustn't concern yourself over how long you'll be staying in my little place."

"I'll pay you rent," I offered. "But I need—"

She shushed me with another pat. "We can work something out, of that I am certain. With everything else that has befallen you, I want this to be the last thing on your mind."

The simple kindness brought a burning to my eyes. "You've been awfully nice, Rachel."

"Nonsense. It's the least I can do." Her eyes lit up as Fred turned through a pair of great stone gates and entered a long tree-lined drive. "Here we are, my dear."

The elms were centuries old and thicker than I was tall. Through the snow-covered boughs I caught glimpses of a house that drew a gasp from my lips. Four stories of stone and turrets and gables and gargoyles, a fantasy palace standing proud and stern in a vast sea of white.

Rachel paid my reaction no mind, nor did Fred. For as we drew up before the vast entrance, the front doors opened, and a sea of little figures came cascading down the stairs. There were so many of them, and they were making so much noise, that I drew back from the door.

Then I saw Fred smiling and rolling down his window to admit a dozen little hands. I watched as Rachel allowed them to draw open her door and engulf her, and I knew my fears were groundless.

The voices were a keening babble as I opened my own door and stepped out. I could not understand a word of what was said. A few of the little ones looked my way, those who were at the periphery of the circle around Rachel. Their outstretched hands formed a skirt of arms extending out from the elderly woman. She responded with a crooning voice and strokes to as many of the faces as she could reach.

She turned to me and called out, "Come along, my dear. We mustn't keep you out in this cold."

"But who are all these children?"

"Ah," she said, moving at a slow enough pace to allow the children to flow with her. "These are my little angels. And the reason I have strength to meet another day."

"THREE HUNDRED CHILDREN?"

"Two hundred and seventy-six, at last count." Rachel's arms were white to the elbow, and a smudge of flour creased her forehead where she had wiped away a stray lock of hair. "But we are scheduled to receive more next week. At least, that is what we were informed the day before yesterday."

I continued to peel the potatoes, just to give my hands something to do. "But who *are* they?"

"War orphans." She had said it before, but the words had not really sunk in. She kept her tone light and musical, as a half dozen little ones were playing a hand-clapping game in the kitchen's far corner. "They come from all over, as far as we have been able to tell. Most of them speak languages that none of us can fathom."

I set down my knife. "They've sent you children without even telling you where they're from?"

"Don't look so concerned, my dear." Rachel almost sang the words. "They can't understand you, so they only hear the tone. And yes, that is exactly the case. From what I've heard, there are some truly horrific discoveries being made over on the Continent."

I nodded, recalling half-heard news stories about camps and trains and things so bad I had always turned away. But now I glanced over to where a half-dozen sets of eyes were observing me. Huge eyes, dark and quietly watchful. Their bodies were little, and the faces so pale and so fragile they seemed barely able to contain those great cautious gazes. I smiled down at them, and tried to match Rachel's light tone. "I don't understand."

"No, I don't suppose you do." She slid out an empty metal tray, dusted it with flour, and began rolling out loaves of dough. Three other women moved about in utter silence. They carried themselves with the stolid determination of people too tired to see or hear beyond the task at hand. Rachel went on, "Neither do we for that matter, not fully. I can only tell you what we ourselves have learned.

"Millions of people are wandering about Europe, from the sound of things. Simply millions. Displaced persons, they're called, DPs for short. And among them are thousands and thousands of orphans. No papers, no explanation for how they got to be where they are, and often no one who understands their language."

Rachel stopped in her work, and stared at the group huddled quietly in the corner. "Several of the officers who were stationed here are now working with the Red Cross on these displaced persons. The plight of these children simply broke their hearts. They decided to turn their vacated War College into a temporary orphanage."

I was unsure which question to ask first. "But you can't even understand them."

One of the other women gave a snort. Rachel glanced her way before replying, "Oh, we have been promised interpreters. We've been promised the moon, for that matter. And no doubt we shall receive them. In time. What matters, however, is how we are going to . . ."

Rachel stopped as the kitchen door was pushed aside by a dark-haired pixie with flashing eyes. The girl raced over, started to take Rachel's hand, and then stopped. Rachel asked, "What is it, Annique?"

The girl was perhaps thirteen or fourteen, quite a bit older than the others I had seen around the ground floor. I had not visited the rest of the house, however. As soon as we had arrived, a harried woman had come racing over and told us to hurry in and start with the kitchen, half of the day crew had failed to show up, what with the snow and it being New Year's, as if the children would understand why they weren't to be fed because the idiots had celebrated too much. The food delivery was late as well, for that matter, so just make do with what we could find. Then she had turned and raced away, her skirts and hair flying.

Rachel had then said to me, "That is probably the only introduction to the mistress of the night shift that you are likely to receive. Her name, by the way, is Kate." As I stood there, more shouted comments had drifted out from somewhere down the back hall. And I had realized the reason behind Kate's hurried commentary was that Rachel ran the day-shift crew.

Rachel asked gently, "Do you need something, Annique?"

But the girl was now staring at me, her dark eyes probing with silent intensity. Then she marched over and grasped my hand. I looked a question at Rachel.

"This is Annique," Rachel explained. "She was found wandering the streets of Munich, more or less in charge of a group of a dozen younger children. That is all we know."

Annique gave my hand a tug and said something in an urgent, sibilant tone. Rachel continued, "Annique is something of a guardian angel for the younger children. You'd best go with her."

I nodded, and allowed myself to be led out of the kitchen and down a long side corridor. Annique was a truly lovely child, despite the shadows and harsh edges that marred her features. She was dressed in a smock far too large for her thin frame, which of course made her look even more emaciated. The fingers and arm that led me were little more than skin and bone, and her face was etched to a fineness that made me shudder to think what she had seen and endured.

She led me up a flight of narrow stairs that had probably been intended for the servants' use, and stopped before a hall cupboard. She pointed at the door, but said nothing. A soft whimpering seemed to be coming from inside the cupboard. I hesitated a moment, then knocked and opened the door. And my heart melted.

Curled up on a stack of starched bed linens was a little boy. He could not have been more than four or five. His hair was the color of honey, and his eyes were big and gray and full of tears. He had all the fingers of one hand crammed into his mouth, I suppose to stop his cries from being heard. He gave me a terrified look, and scrunched up into a tighter little ball.

I reached out my hands to him, but did not touch. Something told me that the first contact needed to come from his side. Annique studied me with an impassive gaze as I spoke words I am sure he did not understand. But I kept talking, and gradually his tears stopped.

Then he reached out one little finger, and touched my open palm, and for some reason I found myself crying as well. The boy unwound enough to let me reach for him and pull him up and in my embrace. He wrapped his thin arms around my neck with a fierce strength, and buried his face in my shoulder.

Annique's reaction surprised me. She studied the pair

of us, then simply nodded and walked away. I stared after her for a moment before starting back toward the kitchen.

In the doorway, I halted once more. There beside Rachel was the young vicar. The two of them were unloading produce from a stack of wooden crates. Rachel looked up and smiled, "Ah, there you are. Crisis resolved?"

Her offhand attitude startled me as much as Annique had. I described what I had found. It was the vicar who replied, "It happens quite a lot, I'm afraid. Goodness only knows what living nightmares these children have endured."

I shifted the boy to my other side. He loosened his grasp only long enough to become resettled, then curled his arms back tightly around me. "But what are we supposed to do?"

"Precisely what you are doing right now," Rachel replied. She waited as the two helpers set yet another huge pot upon the stove and ladled in water. "Give them love."

"They may not understand our words," Reverend Albright agreed. "But they pay the utmost attention to our actions."

He left while I was still mulling that over, and returned with another heavily laden crate. "I think that's the lot," he huffed. "The shipment was short today by half. Snows kept the produce man from making his deliveries, and the village grocers are almost empty."

Rachel was already busy dicing carrots and dropping the segments into the big pot. "And what, may I ask, are these children supposed to eat?"

"The local shops are doing more than their share, and you know it," Colin Albright chided. "Everything we've bought for the past two months has been on account. It's almost enough to break the butcher. I can only hope the Ministry finally comes through with something more than words." He wrapped the scarf back around his neck. "And now I'm off to get the doctor."

Rachel turned to him, a stricken look on her face. "Not another child."

"Two, I'm afraid."

"Still no idea what it is?"

"No, but thankfully he's leaning away from calling it meningitis. It doesn't seem to be as serious as he first thought."

The vicar turned toward me, and in that instant the sun finally managed to break through the clouds. Sunlight lanced through the grimy kitchen window, and fell full force upon Colin Albright's brow. He winced, tightening his face into well-worn lines. He was probably still in his late twenties, but his features were drawn like those of a much older person. He had the grayish pallor of a man limping along the brink of exhaustion. "It is nice to see you again, Miss Robbins."

I nodded as much as the child in my arms would allow, still unsure what to think of this overly tired vicar. When the door had closed behind him, I observed, "If he doesn't sit down, he's going to fall down."

"Colin Albright is the reason we have managed at all," Rachel agreed. "I'm head of the day crew in name only. Colin is director, general, and full-time handyman. He is everywhere, doing everything no one else seems to have time for. I have yet to discover when that man sleeps."

The boy was beginning to grow heavy. I walked over and settled him onto the corner of the long central table. He did not seem to mind, so long as he could keep his arms wrapped around my neck. "I don't understand," I said, and stroked the downy hairs at the nape of his neck. "They just dumped these children on you?"

"Not intentionally, no. We are supposed to be receiving all sorts of assistance. But until they sort things out, we are forced to do the best we can with what we have." She lifted the ladle and tasted the soup she was making. "Mind you, this whole thing has done the village a world of good, if you'd like the opinion of one old woman."

"You're not old," I said automatically. I felt the little arms begin to slacken, and watched as the child unleashed me. The face turned up long enough for me to look into eyes that held the depths of one ten times his age. He gave me a tiny smile, then slipped from the table and was gone.

I stared at the space where he had been. Somehow my heart ached with this sudden passage. I could still feel his arms around me.

When I turned around, I found Rachel staring at me, a tender smile playing upon her face. "Annique was right," she said. "You were exactly what the child needed."

For some reason, Rachel's words left me feeling exposed and uncomfortably vulnerable. I changed the subject. "What did you mean when you said this has been good for the village?"

"Ah," Rachel said, turning back to her steaming pot. "That you will have to discover for yourself."

TEN

Marissa awoke to sunlight and a ringing telephone. She knew instantly it was her mother. She opened her eyes to see Gran roll over and reach for the portable phone. Marissa pleaded, "Don't tell them about last night."

Her eyes on her granddaughter, Gran punched the connection button and said, "Hello?" A moment's pause, then, "Good morning, yes, I'm afraid you did. Marissa—"

"Please," she said, her voice rising an octave.

"Marissa and I got to talking and stayed up half the night," Gran went on. "No, no, she's doing as well as can be expected. Yes, of course I will, just as soon as she's up and about. Of course, Carol. How is everyone? Lovely. And you're having a good time? Good. That's very good. Well, give one and all our love."

She set down the phone, and asked, "Mind if I ask what that was all about?"

"I don't want them to worry," Marissa said, sinking back to her pillow.

Gran rose and crossed the floor. "How are you feeling today?"

"About the same, I guess. Maybe a little better."

"You don't look as pale as last night." Gran brushed the

hair from her forehead. "But maybe we should take our breakfast up here today, what do you think?"

"Okay." It took a genuine effort to raise herself up, stage by stage, until she was standing by the bed. Her grandmother stood ready to assist, but did not reach out, letting her take it as far as she could on her own. Proud that she had managed by herself, Marissa said, "It was hepatitis that they had, wasn't it? The children."

"Ah, now you're getting ahead of the story." Gran walked alongside her as she headed toward the bathroom. "Let me go prepare our breakfast, then I'll come back and tell you what happened next."

GRAN'S STORY

That evening I walked down the lane and turned up the river road. Light splashed out of centuries-old cottages, making the snow shimmer gold. The wind was brisk, and the cold air burned my face. Overhead a few stars managed to shine through clouds chasing across the night sky. The loudest noises were the wind and my scrunching footsteps.

I hesitated a long moment outside the pub's entrance. Once inside, I had no idea what I was going to do. But I could feel the night's icy tendrils creep into my chest, and knew I could stand there no longer.

I pushed through the door, and entered the smoky warmth. There was laughter and the cheerful talk of old friends. I had heard how pubs were a part of English country life, how locals used them as extensions of their own living rooms. At first glance, I understood why lonely airmen might risk life and limb on icy roads to come here.

A roaring fire crackled in a grand stone fireplace, casting a ruddy glow upon the two rooms. Tables darkened by age and hard use were ringed by padded benches and high-backed chairs. The ceilings were beamed and low, the windows tiny blades of leaded glass.

About half the crowd were locals, probably farmers, their faces chapped and roughened by the elements. The others wore uniforms and talked in loud American twangs.

A head at the bar turned my way. I saw eyes widen in genuine apprehension, and recognized the pilot's wings on his shoulders. His gaze grew even wider as I walked straight toward him. My heart was thundering with fear, but seeing how nervous he had become gave me the strength to smile and say, "What's your name?"

"B-Bob McIntyre," he stammered.

I nodded, as though the name meant something to me. I did not introduce myself. Instead, I simply said, "You recognized me from my photo, I suppose."

"Y-yes, ma'am." By this time, all his buddies were staring openly. "I'm real sorry about . . ."

I struggled to force away another bloom of pain in my heart. The bartender chose that moment to walk over and ask if I wanted something. I gave my head a little shake, more of a shudder. He shared a glance with someone behind me, and I knew that all the pub was watching and listening.

I straightened with a determined effort and forced my voice to remain steady. "You know what Grant has done."

He showed the decency to blush. "Yes, ma'am."

And suddenly he was just a young lad, far from home and dumped into a situation that was not of his making. I reached over and patted his arm. "It's all right. Well, not all right, but it's certainly not your fault."

"Grant flew in my squadron for a while," Bob said. He was slender, with red hair and freckles to match. His face was untouched by age or the stress of battle, and he could have easily passed for a teenager except for his uniform. "I never figured him for a guy that'd just cut and run like this."

"No, neither did I. But he did, and I'm trapped here." I explained the difficulty I was facing, trying to find a ship's berth. "I was just wondering if maybe you could help me find a place on one of your flights."

He brightened immensely at the thought of being able to do more than apologize for a vanished friend. "Say, now that you mention it, I might be able to at that. Won't be easy though."

"Sure." A taller soldier with airman's wings shouldered his way up alongside Bob. He spoke with a strong midwestern twang. "We've got air convoys coming through here a couple of times a week. They're chock full to the brim with guys headed home from Europe. And there's a long waiting list of fellows around here, just looking for the empty berth." He gave me a friendly nod. "Name's Bradley Atwater, ma'am. The commander stuck me with these bozos, hopin' I'd be able to keep 'em straight."

"Don't believe a word of it. Brad's the worst of a bad . . ." Bob's flush spread once more, and he swiftly changed the subject. "I bet we could squeeze you in somewhere. That is, if you don't mind waiting around awhile."

"It sounds like I don't have any choice." I smiled my gratitude. "My name is Emily Robbins. I live in Grant's old place. Do you know where that is?"

"Sure, just down there around the corner. We've all been there for . . ." Again he realized where he was headed. Blushing came easy to him and his natural redheaded complexion. He finished lamely, "I know where you live."

"I'm ready to go at any time," I said.

Yet the instant I spoke the words, I felt the strangest tug at my heart. I could not explain it, but there was a sense of the words being utterly untrue. I had no idea what was going on. I was four thousand miles from home, and had absolutely nothing holding me here. But I had the clearest sense that I was not going anywhere.

Bob did not notice this hesitation. He grinned and looked even younger than before. "Don't you worry, ma'am, I mean, Emily. We'll keep an eye peeled for a spot."

"We'll get the paperwork all ready too," offered his buddy. "Least we can do."

"And say, the PX out there at the base is chock full of gear. Anything you need, just give us the word."

"Got all kindsa food and stuff coming out of our ears," confirmed Bradley.

"Thank you, but I'm doing just fine for the moment," I said. Yet again there was the sense of my voice going one way, and my heart another. It was certainly a confusing night. I turned toward the door, giving them a final smile. "I'll be ready to go at the drop of a hat."

I DREAMED OF Grant that night. He was strong and handsome and cheerful as he came back to sweep me up and carry me away. I laughed as I ran toward him, and as I ran I realized that everything I thought had happened to me since my arrival in England had been my imagination. Just a horrible, appalling nightmare. Now he was back, and everything was going to be fine.

My heart seemed to awaken, lifting up with such joy that it threatened to soar out of my chest. I ran toward him, calling his name, singing it out. Grant, oh my Grant. I was running so fast that all the world became a blur, just colors melting together and sweeping along on both sides. My feet truly had wings. I rushed up and leaped into his embrace.

Then I woke up. One moment he was there before me, laughing and holding his arms out to embrace me, and the next I was awake.

The shock was so harsh, so cold and sudden, that I screamed out loud. I rolled from the bed, searching the room not for Grant, but for the dream. Seeing only the dark waiting shadows, the big empty bed, and the snow falling outside my window, I collapsed to the floor. My strength was gone. My heart was broken anew. I just lay in a heap and sobbed.

The only thing that got me up and moving was the

prospect of having to spend a day there alone, with nothing to do but weep. I dressed with numb fingers and went next door. When Rachel answered my knock, I asked, "Are you going to the orphanage this morning?"

"I go every morning," she said, inspecting my face. She seemed to read there everything that had happened. Even the dream. She took hold of my arm and drew me inside. "Come along, my dear. Let me fix you a nice cup of tea."

I did not object. Anything was better than sitting over there alone, surrounded by what would never be. She led me to the kitchen and into a high-backed chair by the little corner table. Her back to me, she said quietly, "A man like Grant will find his own punishment, my dear. Perhaps he already has, you know, in choosing a life without you. What is important is that you must find it in your heart to forgive him."

"Forgive Grant?" I felt as though she had reached over and slapped me. "I couldn't. Not ever."

"Well, until you do, you will not find peace." When I did not respond, she continued in a voice that was very low, very soft. "I did not go back to church for a very long time after Samuel's funeral. I couldn't. Well, I did once, about three weeks after we laid him to rest. As I entered, I heard a voice speak directly to my heart, commanding me to forgive. But I couldn't forgive. Not God, and certainly not the people who were responsible for my boy's . . ."

Rachel fell silent. She finished preparing my tea, and set the cup down in front of me. She seated herself in the other chair, folded her hands determinedly in her lap, and continued quietly, "Finally I went back because I had to. My heart was a vacuum, a void just waiting to be filled. A lifetime of grief and hatred was a temptation I could not keep away, not on my own. It would have been so easy, so utterly agreeable, to enter the Grim Brigade. But of course, once I did I would have been lost forever."

I found myself remembering the New Year's Eve service, and seeing those shadowy faces take form. There in her cheerful little kitchen, I had a sudden waking dream. Perhaps it was the force of experience behind her words. Perhaps it was my own grief-stricken state. Whatever the reason, once again I found myself staring through the darkness and the snowfall, only this time I was standing right there in line with the other bitter, hate-ridden faces.

Rachel was too lost in her memories to notice my shudder. "That was what drove me back to church, not any desire to seek God's comfort. I woke up one Sabbath morning, and recalled the passage in Scripture where a demon found the house swept clean and left empty, so he went and gathered seven of his fellows, all worse than himself, and came back with them and possessed the soul."

I remembered that passage. I recalled sitting in church one sunny morning and hearing the pastor of my youth speak those words. I remembered how comforted I was to be sitting there, surrounded by friends and family, knowing that God was there in His house, and I would be kept safe. And now? I studied Rachel's face, and saw an extraordinary mixture of strength and weakness, age and youth, sadness and joy. And wisdom. There was such wisdom to that quiet voice that it rang like great silver bells within my heart.

"That morning," Rachel went on, "Colin Albright was giving the sermon. I have no idea what he spoke about. I sat there, and felt that even within the church I was not beyond the reach of all that had driven me from the house. Then, through the fog that had wrapped itself around my mind and heart, one passage managed to work through to me. Eight little words Colin spoke, that's all I heard. But it was enough."

When Rachel remained silent, I found my voice and asked, "What did he say?"

She looked at me then, her eyes filled with a sadness that reached across the gulf of years and nationalities and different sorrows. She said, "Even the pagans love those who love them."

Slowly I gave a nod. I remembered that passage as well. It was when the Lord had said that we must love our enemies. That was what would set us apart from all others. The message was a crushing challenge. And suddenly I was crying. Sobbing without control. I heard Rachel rise and come to me, I felt her touch my cheek, my neck, then slide around to hold me close, offering me a comfort beyond words.

Finally I was able to regain enough control to accept the handkerchief she offered. I whispered, "I don't know if I can ever do that. Forgive Grant, I mean."

"I know." Her murmur was almost as soft as my own. "But allow the Lord's gentle grace to enter your wounded spirit, my dear, and He will work the miracle for you Himself."

ELEVEN

Oh, do get a move on, Fred," Rachel complained from the taxi's backseat. "I might as well have walked."

"You can step out and try anytime you like." He kept his nose pressed to the cracked windscreen. Snow billowed and swirled outside, reducing vision to barely a few feet beyond the car's hood. "Don't see how anybody's going much of anywhere today."

"Don't say that," Rachel said, her tone rising with sudden tension. "The thought kept me awake all night."

"Heard on the wireless most of the trains out this way have been canceled," Fred went on. "No help from that corner."

I looked from one to the other. "What's the matter?"

As Rachel opened her mouth to respond, the snow eased momentarily, revealing the startling sight of the road simply ending in a high white embankment. Fred jerked the wheel around hard. The taxi spun wildly, before doing a four-wheel slide through the great stone gates. "Sorry, ladies. Heard before I left this morning, the council only cleared the roads as far up as the College. Took 'em the better part of four hours to get this far."

Rachel turned to stare through the snow-spattered back

windscreen, and wailed, "But how are the deliveries supposed to get through?"

"Been asking myself that same question all morning," Fred said worriedly. He wheeled up in front of the imposing house and stopped. "This is my last trip of the day, ladies. You'll have to ask the vicar to bring you home. That old heap of his has four-wheel drive. He'll get you back safe and sound."

Rachel paid and stepped from the taxi. She stood and seemed to sniff the air before declaring, "It is far too quiet."

"The snow's keeping everybody inside."

"That's not it," she said emphatically, and stumped up the stairs. "Something's amiss. I just know it."

The grand entrance hall was equally quiet. Rachel slammed the door hard, and hallooed. The sound of her voice echoed eerily. Steps were heard in the distance, a door slammed, another, and then the harried night-mistress came hustling down the back hallway. Kate stopped when she saw who it was, her face falling. "Oh, I hoped it was the grocer."

"Don't tell me he hasn't been here yet."

Kate wrung her hands. "Oh, Rachel, it's like our worst nightmare has come to life. I've been on the phone to the Ministry a half-dozen times already. All deliveries north of London have been halted. They're trying to organize something by train, but there's trouble with them as well, something about the snow having frozen hard to the tracks; I wasn't listening by that point."

"But how are we supposed to feed the children?"

"Precisely what I've been asking the Ministry. All they could tell me was they were working on it." She snorted. "If it's anything like the rate of progress we've seen so far, we'll still be waiting next Christmas."

"Don't say that," Rachel admonished. "Don't even think it."

I asked, "Where are the children?"

"Oh, they're hiding. They know something's the matter, they don't know what it is, but they're hiding just the same."

"I haven't heard it this quiet since we ousted Matilda," Rachel said, glancing around. "Well, what on earth are we to do?"

"Colin's going to try to make it to the next village, bless his heart. He's spoken to the vicar, and they've promised to take up a collection. He's—"

Footsteps clomped down the stairs. Colin Albright came into view, his feet stuffed into great rubber boots. He was wrapping a long gray scarf around his neck and face. "I'm off. Don't get your hopes up, John was not optimistic. They haven't had any deliveries over there either."

"Anything you can get will be better than what we have," Kate replied.

Rachel's face was a mask of concern. "There's nothing at all?"

"A mouthful or two for each child. Colin brought in absolutely everything the local grocers could spare. We found some old potatoes downstairs in the root cellar, and there are some bitter herbs and a few leeks." The woman smiled tiredly. "Most of these children have managed on far less, I'd wager."

"Not while they've been under my care," Colin said grimly. "I'll be back as soon as I can."

"Wait," I said, stepping forward. All eyes turned toward me. "I think I have an idea. Can you drive me to the airfield?"

"My dear," Rachel admonished, "this is hardly the time—"

"I met with a couple of the fliers last night," I said quickly. "They offered me supplies from the PX."

A breathless intake of hope caught them all. "Do you think they really meant it?"

"He said the PX was chock full of stuff," I replied. "Those were his exact words."

"My truck has no heat," Colin warned. "You'll need to wrap up warmer than that to manage a journey over the Chilterns."

THANKFULLY, THE SNOW had eased before we left the village behind. Colin Albright's truck was an old army model, short and set up on a high suspension, so that it looked like a landlocked boat. It rocked dangerously over every dip and sway in the road. But the tires bit easily through the snow, and the engine growled cheerfully as we began to climb.

"Rationing has become such a way of life for us, we can

hardly remember anything else," Colin was saying. His voice came out slightly muffled from behind his tightly wrapped scarf. He had instructed me to do the same—not only because of the cold, but because the wool caught most of the moisture so the windscreen did not freeze up so quickly. "I haven't had chocolate in over a year. We got in a shipment just before Christmas, but you know how it is with children. I got more joy out of watching their faces than I could ever have from eating it myself."

My feet were encased in two pairs of thick woolen socks, then stuffed in those high rubber boots the English called wellies. I wore a pair of men's woolen mittens and my own gloves under them.

Rachel had found me some woolen underwear, far too excited over the prospect of gaining supplies from the Americans to notice my embarrassment. I wore another helper's sweater, my own coat, and a thick woolen cap and scarf from the orphanage's rummage chest. The layers were so thick my arms felt cocked out at angles, like a winter scarecrow. I could scarcely move. The wool itched everywhere it touched—my elbows, under my arms, my forehead, behind my knees, my toes. All that was visible were my eyes. But I was warm, and the drive was exhilarating.

"The only way we've been able to make this project work is because everyone in the village has pitched in," Colin went on, his tone matter-of-fact. "That is, almost everyone. My petrol is coming off an account with the local station. Everything we use is on account—the heating oil, produce, the canned goods, everything. All the clothes you see the children wear. Our meat comes from local butchers and nearby farmhouses that otherwise would have kept it as extra for their own families."

Gradually what I was hearing began to sink in. I turned from watching the village drop away below us, and gazed at this tired-looking vicar beside me. Colin continued, "The government has managed to give everybody just barely enough by rationing almost everything. To have a village our size be forced to support three hundred orphans has put a strain on everyone."

"But the war is over," I protested.

He smiled. "You'll hear a lot of people around here making the same observation. A lot of good it does them."

I turned back to my window, sorting through what I had just heard. I then recalled what Rachel had said the day before, how the orphans' arrival had been the best thing that could have happened to Arden. "It must be hard."

"We manage." His calm tone was belied by the strain and the fatigue in his face. "Barely, but we manage. We keep hoping that the promised help will arrive soon. That, more than anything, keeps us going."

Outside my window, the road was growing steeper. Snow swirled in lazy clouds, opening every once in a while to reveal vistas of white and black and gray. Trees were simple etchings of stark limbs and ancient trunks. Hillsides were decorated with primitive stone cottages and long lines of hedgerows separating empty fields. Then the snow closed in once more, and all was white. "I can't believe they would just dump all those children on you."

"Oh, they gave us help. Initially." His voice turned as stark as the winter white beyond our little cab. "Her name was Matilda Whetlock. You will hear that name spoken with dread by all who met her. Prior to her arrival in Arden, she ran a borstal."

"A what?"

"A prison. A borstal for young women. She was hard as nails, Matilda was. She and the staff she'd brought along with her. A worse caretaker for children coming from the horrors of war I could not possibly imagine."

Outrage filled his voice. "We were positively aghast at what we saw happening. The children were so terrified of her and the staff, they neither ate nor slept. We would arrive most mornings to find them sleeping outdoors, rather than be put to bed by Matilda Whetlock. We spent most of August and September walking from tree to tree, gathering up these little forms, then battling the mistress and her staff to keep them from punishing our children."

He stopped the truck right in the middle of the road. There was no need to pull off to one side. There was no traffic. The road was an unblemished strip of white, thankfully marked by hedgerows and low stone walls. Otherwise there would have been no way to tell where the road stopped and the neighboring fields began. Colin walked around front and scraped ice off the windscreen, then returned to the cab and did the same to the inside. He settled back behind the wheel, put the truck into gear, and started off.

When he drove on in silence, I demanded, "What happened?"

"What? Oh, to Matilda, yes, of course. Sorry, I was busy hoping this trip wasn't in vain. We drove her off."

"Who did?"

"The entire village. By that point, everyone within twenty miles was talking about Matilda Whetlock. Her name was enough to give the young ones nightmares, just listening to how the adults spoke of her. We held a town meeting, then went up one day and drove her away, her and her minions." He turned to flash me an apologetic smile. "Which partly explains why the Ministry has been somewhat reluctant to jump in once more. Our actions made the national press. British officialdom does not like to have its hand slapped in public."

"But they have to help you," I cried.

"Oh, they will. But they are dragging their heels in best bureaucratic fashion. It is their way of punishing us, I suppose." He crested the steepest rise so far, and applied the brakes. The truck shuddered to a halt. "Well, the worst is behind us."

He climbed from the truck to give the glass another scraping. As he did, the snow stopped once more. A lance of sunlight managed to break through the clouds. I opened my door and climbed down. When I turned around, and saw where we had come from, I had to grip the truck for support.

The view was beautiful but frightening. Behind us, the road dipped into a valley of white and silence. Dark gray lines crisscrossed the empty fields, and smoke rose in lazy ribbons from cottages that seemed a very long way below us. "I'm glad I didn't know where you were taking me."

Colin Albright laughed, and suddenly the years and the strain fell away. "It is quite a feat, what we've just done. I don't mind saying so myself." He pointed ahead of us. "You can see the airfield in the valley just along there."

The descent was far more gradual than the rise we had just crested. The planes were tiny toys, and the field itself was a long white ribbon laid upon the valley's floor. All was silent and still. Not a person could be seen moving about. I climbed back inside with Colin, exhilarated by the air and the accomplishment. I took an overdeep breath and coughed.

Colin was instantly concerned. "How are you feeling?"

I waved away his concern, fighting to regain my breath. "Fine," I gasped.

"You don't sound fine. You sound like our journey has brought on a relapse."

"Really, it's nothing." I fought down another rising cough, swallowed noisily, and forced out a smile. "I'm on the mend, as Rachel says. Better than that. It's just this silly cough that won't go away."

He did not start forward. Instead, his concerned gaze remained on me. "I really must apologize for that day in the hospital. I was awful."

"No more so than I was," I replied, suddenly glad that it was out in the open.

"You had every reason to say what you did. But the children . . ." He sighed and shook his head. "They had started dropping like flies that very week. No explanation for it, none at all. Suddenly they were just not getting out of bed. Sleeping all the time, their little bellies swelling up, moaning in tongues none of us could understand."

I was glad the scarf disguised my blushing flood of shame. There in the hospital, trapped within my own selfish misery, I had scalded an innocent man with my anger. I felt so small. "I'm sorry," I said weakly. "I didn't know."

"No, of course not, how could you?" But his worry held him, and the words were spoken automatically. "A few of the children are finally growing better. Almost despite our best efforts, or so it seems."

"What do you think it might be?"

"We're not sure." He put the truck into gear. "All we can say for certain is that we can see some improvement, and fewer seem to be falling ill."

As we approached the airfield, round-roof igloos became metal Quonset huts covered in snow. Men began streaming out the doors, drawn by the grinding sound of our motor disturbing the valley's silence. When Colin pulled up and stopped, I shyly stepped down into the snow, pulling away the scarf and cap, searching for a familiar face.

"Miss Robbins!" A red-haired young man came bounding forth, his leather flyer's jacket flapping open to the cold. "What on earth are you doing here?"

"Hello, Bob. Call me Emily, please." I ruffled my hair from the matting it had received inside the woolen cap. "I'd like to introduce Reverend Colin Albright. He's the local vicar."

"Sure, hey, Reverend. I've seen you around."

Bradley Atwater waved and called as he approached, "There ain't no planes today, Emily. Not in, not out."

"Whole world's snowed in," Bob confirmed. "Word is, we're seeing the worst winter in Europe's history."

"I didn't come for myself," I said, reddening under the multitude of gazes. "That is, well," I stopped, took a deep breath, and said, "We desperately need your help."

TWO HOURS LATER, I climbed back into the truck, so full of canned pineapple juice and turkey sandwiches I could scarcely move. "I can't thank you enough, Bob."

"Shoot, Emily, you kidding? Get a load of the guys." Three jeeps were piled high with all the supplies our own vehicle could not carry. Around them, heated arguments rose as men vied for the chance to drive them back to town. "We're just sitting around here, playing cards and jawing, bored to tears."

Bradley Atwater grinned at all and sundry. "Then up pops the cute little lady here, and says we got a load of kids starving to death."

"Well, I'd hardly call it that," Colin murmured.

"Close enough," Bob said, winking at me. "That's what we'll tell the guys at Stores, if anybody tries to raise a stink."

"Probably won't even miss it," Brad offered.

"I would never wish to be party to a lie," Colin said. "But in all honesty, if the snow holds for another few days, it might actually bring us close to starving." Colin offered them his hand. "Be that as it may, we simply cannot thank you enough. All of you."

"Shoot, Reverend, it's a pleasure." Brad was of Indiana farming stock, tall and angular and possessing the jaw of an ox. His midwestern twang rang strong and clear in the icy air. "But you folks better be getting on, looks like it's gonna snow again 'fore too long."

"Right you are." Colin climbed on board and ground the starter. The sound was enough to galvanize those gathered around the jeeps into action. A trio of men stopped the quarreling by being the first three to scramble behind the wheels. There was no room for others. The jump seats were piled high with cartons of canned goods.

"Oh, hey." Bob stepped aside, revealing a box and two lumpy sacks by his feet. "Thought you might use these."

Colin inspected the bags' labels, and his eyes turned round. "It can't be."

"The best there is, and ever will be," Bob agreed proudly. "Real Florida oranges."

"No, really," Colin said, dragging his eyes away from the burlap sacks with their bright yellow emblems. "I simply couldn't."

"Sure you could." Bob waved cheerily as one of the jeeps blew its horn. "They dumped half a ton of this stuff on us. We eat much more, we'll be sick as little puppies."

"Give Emily the other box," Brad urged.

"Yeah, right." His face turned the color of his hair as he lifted the cardboard container. It was very light, given its size. "This is from me and the boys."

"Don't open it now," Brad warned, "otherwise he'll burst into flames."

"We just wanted to tell you," Bob glanced at his friend for support. "Well, ma'am, Miss Robbins . . ."

"The name's Emily," Brad offered cheerfully. "And she already knows that."

He wheeled around. "You mind?"

Brad offered a huge grin and open palms. "Just trying to get this show on the road, pardner."

"Give me a sec." Bob turned back around. "What we wanted to tell you, Emily, is that Grant is a fool."

"The purebred, ten-gallon variety," Brad affirmed.

I felt my face turn a shade to match Bob's. "Thank you," I said weakly.

"Lady as easy to look at as you," Bob went on determinedly, "good-hearted to boot, you deserve better treatment."

"Doggone right," Brad agreed. "Anytime you want to give another flyboy a try, give us a holler."

"Not a chance in this world," I said, glad for a reason to smile. "But thank you just the same."

We settled the sacks on the floor by my feet, and put the box on the seat between us. The men left behind saw us off with a chorus of waves and shouts. The jeeps fell in, one in front and two behind. Once we were well under way, Colin asked me what was in the box. I peeled back the lid and exclaimed, "Silk stockings!"

"An entire *box* of them?" He slowed to gape. "I don't think I've seen a *box* of stockings since the war started."

I closed the lid. "You take them."

He halted so abruptly the jeep behind us did a four-wheel slide up alongside. A voice shouted over, "Hey, what gives!"

"Sorry!" Colin called back, then returned his gaze to me. "Do you have any idea what they are worth?"

"Take them," I repeated. "What on earth am I going to do with that many? Besides, this trip was supposed to be for the children. Maybe you can barter them for something more useful."

"There's no 'maybe' about that." He gave me a long glance. "For what it's worth, I'd like to say that I agree wholeheartedly with the gentlemen's comments about your fiancé's departure."

"Ex-fiancé," I corrected. "But thank you for the sentiment."

I settled back in the seat. The smile I wore seemed to stretch my face into unaccustomed angles.

TWELVE

Marissa entered the kitchen, her face wreathed in smiles. Her hand hovered alongside the door frame, but she stood unsupported. Her beaming face wore a freshly scrubbed shine. Beneath her robe she wore a sweatshirt and stretch pants instead of the nightgown.

She waited for her grandmother to turn around and notice. But Gran moved about the kitchen in noisy concentration, her face one big frown. Gradually Marissa's smile slipped away.

Gran chose that moment to glance over. "Oh, good morning, child." There was none of the hoped-for cheer. Instead, Gran's customary abruptness was sharpened. "Ready for breakfast?"

"I guess so." Glumly, Marissa walked over and seated herself in the breakfast nook. A good deal of the light had gone from the day.

Gran prepared their oatmeal in silence. It was only when she brought over the two steaming bowls that she focused upon Marissa's form, and demanded, "What are you wearing?"

Marissa shrugged. "I felt like dressing for a change."

"That means your energy is returning." A trace of Gran's affection surfaced. "Honey, that's marvelous!"

Marissa tasted her oatmeal. "Have I done something to make you mad at me?"

"Oh, child." Gran set down her spoon. "There are no secrets between us, are there?"

"It wasn't hard to spot." The cinnamon tingled in her mouth and nose. As far back as she could remember, cinnamon and brown sugar were the scents of winter mornings. "What did I do?"

"It's not you, child, not at all." The grim lines deepened the furrows on Gran's face, aging her into a hard-eyed stranger. "I'm just angry with Colin."

"At Granpa?" Incredulous, Marissa stared across the table. "But he's dead."

"Exactly. He's left me here all alone." The eyes glistened as she rapped her spoon on the tabletop. "How *dare* he go off without me and leave me here by myself!"

"You're not alone, Gran," Marissa whispered.

The old lady could no longer remain seated. She rose and paced back into the kitchen. "Oh, I know that, darling. It's just this talking has made the memories of all we shared so much more vivid. I lay awake last night missing him more than I have since the funeral."

Although it cost her dearly, Marissa offered quietly, "You don't have to tell me any more of your story if you don't want to."

Gran stood by the kitchen window for a very long moment. Long enough, in fact, for Marissa's heart to sink with apprehension that she might never know what happened to the orphanage and her grandparents' early days.

But eventually Gran shook her head, and sighed, "No, that wouldn't be right. I've started this, and I want to finish."

"But—"

"Not just for you, child." Slowly Gran walked back over and seated herself. With careful motions she pushed the bowl aside and folded one hand upon the other. "This is for me as well. I believe this to be a very important exercise. I am setting my house in order, you see. I am allowing the most important lessons of my early life to be passed on."

"I really want to hear what happened," Marissa offered.

Gran smiled for the first time that day, and the sudden aging slipped away. "Then hear you shall. Now eat your oatmeal before it grows stone-cold, and let me see if I can remember what happened next."

GRAN'S STORY

Nobody at the orphanage dared touch my box of stockings. There were thirty-six pairs in all, and occasionally I would find a couple of the ladies gathered about the cupboard where they were stored, passing them from hand to hand. Without any discussion, at least not any that I heard, the stockings had been set aside as a sort of barter-savings for a rainy day.

Five days later, the snows finally ended, and the skies cleared. That same afternoon we received some real help from the Ministry, in the form of six lorry-loads of much-needed goods. Shoes and clothes and blankets and sheets and canned goods and soap and cleaning utensils, all the things that one never thinks about until they are not there. The people who helped staff the orphanage walked around in a daze, unable to take in the sudden flood of wealth.

The first thing we did, after storing away most of our goods, was to scour the kitchen. Perhaps they should have done it earlier, but I certainly did not have the heart to point that out. They had been so exhausted, those villagers, from the daily strain of finding enough to feed and clothe the children, that such things as fighting infection had simply been postponed.

Every utensil was boiled and then boiled again. The floors and walls and stoves and counters were scrubbed with wire brushes and disinfectant. The beds were stripped, the mattresses scrubbed, and the sheets boiled in lye. The entire house stank of carbolic acid, and we ate in the far downstairs room for four days. And we waited. The doctors had finally decided the children probably had hepatitis, the signal being that those who got better stayed so. If it was indeed hepatitis, we should now begin to see a decline in the infection rate.

By the end of that second week, I was working at the orphanage more or less full-time, and thinking of the children as ours. For as long as I needed to stay in England, I was united with the villagers by the needs of these wonderful children. And they truly were wonderful.

The brightest among them, and those who had been least scarred, had begun to pick up their first words of English. We could not organize classes, there simply was too much work and too few volunteers. We also had neither books nor blackboard nor enough pencils and paper to go around. It did not matter. The children gathered whenever there was an adult or two with free time, and they learned the words for everything within reach, everything they could see through the windows, everything we could find in chattering parades through the grand old house. We sang hymns, the children mouthing words that meant little or nothing to them, but loving it all the same.

Annique continued to seek me out, pulling me down hallways and up back stairwells, chattering softly in a tongue I could not understand, drawing me to little forms huddled in attics and closets and crannies.

My health continued to improve. The warm spell helped tremendously. I was able to get out some afternoons and walk through the manor's huge estate. After five years of neglect, the formal gardens had become overrun. But I found the leaf-strewn paths to be even more beautiful for their unkempt state. It was a private place, where I could draw out my problems and my woes, and inspect them in peace. I found myself healing, both inside and out.

Later that week the doctors confirmed what we had been hoping. The rate of infection was slowing. But with the good news came the bad; it was not slowing as fast as it should.

As a result, Colin and I made a second trip out to the Arden airfield. This was a very different trip indeed. The road was awash in icy rivulets, the sky china blue. Although the fields were still winter brown and dotted with snow, our stop at the top of the rise rang with the sounds of life. I took in great breaths of the clear country air, and listened to the chorus of sheep, cows, chickens, and children from the valley below.

"The trouble with stopping out here is I never want to leave," Colin confessed.

"It is beautiful," I agreed. I was becoming increasingly comfortable with the soft-spoken assistant vicar. Colin was an odd candidate for sainthood, with his shock of sandy hair that looked as though it had never seen a brush, and his utter disregard for the state of his clothes or his truck. He often forgot to eat, unless someone grabbed hold as he rushed by and sternly ordered him to sit. He was scatterbrained and forgetful, and he took on more work than could possibly have been handled by two men.

But the children loved him, and he kept up a determined effort never to let them down. We would work together for hours, scrubbing floors, or making vast urns of soup, or tending the sick children, and scarcely share a word. Yet just being around Colin Albright was helping to heal my wounds. His silence and his dependability assured me that not all men were like Grant.

Once again, our truck's arrival caused a mad scramble around the airfield. Brad, the Indiana farmboy, separated himself from the rush to greet us with a grand wave. "Was wondering when you folks'd show up again."

"I'm awfully sorry that we only come when we need something," Colin said, stepping down from his truck.

"Shoot. We been wondering why you haven't come back

before now." He tipped his airman's cap in my direction. "Bob's off on a jaunt across the Atlantic, Emily. But we haven't forgotten you. Just been awful tied up lately. Planes have been in here morning, noon, and night, what with this spell of nice weather. Kept us all hopping. Ain't had a single spare seat, though. I've been watching."

"That's okay," I said, extending my smile to all the gathered young men. It was becoming increasingly easy to smile these days. "I've been pretty busy myself."

"She's proved herself to be indispensable to our efforts," Colin agreed.

"So how come you haven't been back for more stuff, Reverend?"

Colin found it hard to respond. "Actually, we've hardly ever asked for anything."

"Come again?"

"Well, you see, we've rarely made collections even among the villagers, that is, unless there has been a genuine emergency."

"Like now," I added.

"Precisely. The villagers have simply given what they could, and we have tried to make do."

For some reason, the vicar's words seemed to shame the tall young man. "All this time, we been standing around here like a buncha jackdaws," he muttered. "Wait till Bob hears about this."

"You really mustn't think like that," Colin protested. "Your largesse in our hour of need was a godsend."

"Yeah, well, we coulda done more."

It seemed like a perfect opportunity to discuss our plight. "We have a problem," I said, and told him of the children's illness. "We're not sure, but the doctors think it's probably hepatitis. We want to inoculate those who are well, and the Ministry has promised us the drug . . ." I looked helplessly at Colin. I had forgotten the word.

"Gamma globulin," he supplied. "But we've been waiting for weeks now, and still they say there is nothing available. I fear there are other afflicted areas with higher priority than an orphanage full of foreigners."

"Not as far as we're concerned." Brad turned and shouted, "Where's Smitty?"

"Here." A bowlegged ox dressed only in a green T-shirt and fatigues, despite the cold, emerged from the crowd. "How many kids we talking about?"

"One hundred and seventy are well," I replied. "Another hundred and nineteen are bedridden."

"Not a hope," Smitty replied. "I got maybe two dozen doses."

"We'll get more," Brad declared, and levered his jaw out another determined inch. "Or my name ain't Bradley Atwater."

Once again, the truck was overloaded for the return journey. Our protests were simply ignored as a steady stream of young men carried out box after box of PX canned goods. Finally we gave up, and allowed ourselves to be herded inside their warehouse.

We walked the aisles in stunned silence. I had forgotten how different things were back home. I found myself thinking of the Arden village grocer's empty shelves. Or the arguments relayed by one of the helpers who had gone in to ask the butcher for soup bones. Or the rationing of everything from sugar to dresses. Or how at least once a week the baker had no flour with which to make bread. The amount of goods in this warehouse, stacked right to the ceiling, seemed vaguely obscene.

We allowed ourselves to select two cases of canned meat, and four more of orange juice. From an entire aisle of medical supplies we chose bandages and aspirin and ointments and iodine and cough medicine. Our quiet excitement caused the young men accompanying us to beam like lighthouses. As we started back toward the truck, Brad stopped at the corner.

"Oh, hey. I almost forgot. Think you could use any of these?"

I had been too excited until then to notice, but the smell hit me hard. I did not need to see what Brad was holding up. I stepped over to the open door, hoping the fresh air would relieve my sudden nausea.

Colin's reaction could not have been more different. "Bananas," he said, his voice hushed. "You must be joking."

"We got three hundred pounds of the things dumped on us last week. Been eating 'em like we're racing the clock. Got 'em coming outta our ears."

"May I?" Reverentially, Colin pulled one off the stem, peeled it, and took a bite. He closed his eyes as he chewed. Finally he said, "I haven't had a banana in four years. No, make that five."

"Do us all a favor, Reverend." Brad extended the armload. "Take these things off our hands, will you?"

"With pleasure." Colin handled the gift as he would the sacraments. "I doubt many of these children have ever tasted a banana."

The words brought a sudden stillness to the gathering. The smiles vanished. "You serious?"

"Totally." Colin took the last bite of his fruit. "That was perfectly delicious. Thank you so much."

Another moment's silence, then Smitty offered, "Supposed to get in another load of oranges next week."

"We will take whatever you don't need yourselves," Colin said. "Certainly."

The bananas were loaded in a strangely subdued silence. It was not until we were inside and Brad climbed on the running board, that he explained, "Most of the guys, they're using this extra junk to, well . . ."

"Impress the local ladies," Colin replied quietly. "I quite understand."

"I don't guess any of us thought maybe we should do something on our own, you know, without somebody asking for help." He stood there and continued to chew on his lip for a while before confessing, "Our chaplain, he got shipped back in November."

"Yes, I know. He was a friend of mine," Colin said quietly. "Well, it certainly would be an honor to have you and all your friends join us for our Sunday service."

"That might just be the ticket." Brad shot me a quick

glance from beneath his heavy black brows. "We sorta been hanging around too much lately."

"Don't be too hard on yourselves," Colin said. "You have all been through the ravages of war. It's perfectly natural that you would want to blow off some steam." He hesitated, then added, "But I would appreciate your not repeating my words to the fathers of our village maidens."

Brad grinned through the open window. "You're all right, Reverend."

"A rare and valuable compliment indeed," Colin said, returning the smile. "I would only counsel you and your friends to remember the Scriptures as you unwind."

Brad nodded slowly. "I believe I'll take you up on your offer to visit you in church. Some things I've sorta let slide."

"Excellent." Colin ground the starter. "Until Sunday, then."

We drove the entire way back in silence, my window lowered a bit to keep the smell of ripening bananas from overwhelming me. Occasionally we glanced at each other and shared a smile. For some reason, the visit to the airfield had left us both feeling things that simply could not be put into words.

THIRTEEN

The next morning I awoke to the sound of heavy rain drumming on my clay-tiled roof. Once again, I had dreamed about Grant. For the first time since the early days of my illness, I had difficulty rising from my bed. Tendrils of my dreams held me like rank and odiferous roots. They had grown up about me in the night, and now sought to draw me down into the dark and bitter earth.

As quickly as I could manage, I dressed and walked next door. My eyes remained dry, but my heart was sore from the memories reawakened by the dream. The rain fell in steady sheets. As I let myself in to Rachel's house with the key she had given me, I had the feeling that the sky was crying for me.

We had fallen into the habit of breakfasting together. I tried to dredge up a smile in reply to her cheery hello. I accepted a cup of tea sweetened with condensed milk from the PX, one of the few things Rachel had taken for herself, and confessed, "I dreamed about Grant again last night."

"Yes, well, it happens." Rachel popped toast into the oven, and stood sipping her cup at the counter. "If only we could cauterize our hearts and memories like we can our body's wounds."

I nodded, but in truth I was thinking about the dream. How Grant had walked strange streets I knew belonged to Berlin, searching for me, calling my name, confused because I was not there with him. "Do you think maybe I should go to Berlin, and just give—"

"No, I most certainly do not." Her tone was quiet yet firm. "Grant is no longer a part of your life, my dear. For better or worse, he has chosen his course. You must free yourself, and look to your own future."

Though it was hard to accept the words, I liked Rachel's way of neither excusing nor pushing aside, but accepting with a quiet dignity and strength. It appealed to me. There was no falseness in her way of discussing Grant. He was who he was, he had done what he did. "You're right," I sighed. "It's just, well . . ."

"You miss him," she said matter-of-factly. "But you must not mistake your heart's whimper as a call from either God or a possible future. That door is closed."

After breakfast, we spent the few final minutes before the taxi arrived standing out on Rachel's balcony. The row of houses had originally been one long riverside inn. When the industrial revolution made travel affordable for most people, Arden had become a favorite destination. It lay midway between Oxford and London, and families would come here to escape the city's confines. They would overnight here and spend the next day cruising up and down the Thames on long Victorian steam launches.

That morning, the heavy rain turned the sky the same color as the slate-gray river. Across the water, a narrow field stretched to meet hills that rose in lazy ridges. The vista was very sleepy-looking, decorated by forests stripped bare in winter, and by the rain. The loudest sounds were the calls of geese who wintered on the plain, and lorries trundling across the ancient stone bridge to my right.

"I love to come out here," Rachel murmured, "and listen to the river."

The breeze flicked rain back to where I stood by the door. "It's cold."

"Perhaps." Rachel did not move. "I only notice it until I hear the river speak to me. After that, the unspoken truths warm me to the core."

She glanced over at me, a contented smile playing upon her features. "I find God's creation holds so many lessons. From this little stretch of river I have learned the power of those simple words, 'Be still and know.' It is only when I learn to quiet my mind and heart that I can sometimes catch the faintest hint of what can never be expressed in words alone."

I stood beside her, watching the water sweep by below us. Light and wind and rain sent scattered impressions across the surface, coming and going so swiftly they melded into one giant intangible canvas.

When the doorbell sounded, I was glad to turn away and follow Rachel back inside. I felt my eyes had been shown what my heart was not yet ready to fathom.

When Fred dropped us off at the orphanage, the night-mistress came rattling down the stairwell to greet us. She had taken to wearing a great ring of keys strapped to her belt, one for the main doors and others for each of the larders, which were becoming increasingly full. With each step, Kate jangled like an old-fashioned potsherd.

"Annique is down," she said in greeting, speaking to me and not to Rachel. "And she's calling for you."

I felt a hand rise to catch my lurching heart. "What do you mean, 'down'?"

Impatiently she grasped my arm and tugged me upstairs. "I mean she's down, what do you think?"

"But she can't be," I protested, allowing myself to be dragged to the upstairs sick-hall. "The children are getting better."

"And I'm telling you she woke up with a swollen liver and a jaundiced complexion," Kate replied edgily. Nights of interrupted sleep were taking their toll. "She should be sleeping, but all she does is lie there and cry for her *Andiel* Emily."

"Andiel? What's that?"

"I haven't the foggiest."

The upstairs ballroom had been transformed into an isolation hall. The grand domed ceiling, with the ceramic cherubs in each corner and the trio of crystal chandeliers, now looked down over a hundred little forms. There were beds of every variety, from farm cots with straw mattresses to cast-off whitewashed hospital beds to one ancient four-poster holding three of the smaller children. The hall smelled of disinfectant and illness.

As soon as the door opened, I heard a familiar high-pitched voice calling weakly. I rushed down the long central aisle until I arrived at Annique's bed. Two spindly arms were outstretched, the bright dark eyes imploring me with a language that I could understand. I sank to the bedside, and allowed the arms to draw me close. As I held her, I realized it was the first time I had ever touched more than her hand.

Annique was always there, playing the little assistant, guiding me to those in need, watching as I held and comforted. But she had never let me embrace her. Now, as I spoke soothing words and stroked the fine black hair, I realized that watching others receive affection was as close as Annique had permitted another person to come, until now.

I sat there and rocked Annique back and forth. Time seemed to slow, and the outside world receded. I found myself thinking back to standing upon Rachel's balcony.

I remembered the river's gentle flowing, and the sound of the rain, and the way the calm had tried to work its way into my bruised and battered spirit. *Peace, be still,* came the whispered words to my heart. As though it was only now, when need forced me to reach inside and tap my own inner well, that I was able to hear the silent voice.

I do not know how long I sat there holding Annique. But finally a hand touched my shoulder, and a voice said, "There is a telephone call for you."

"For me?" I turned and stared up at one of the sick-hall helpers. "But nobody knows I'm here."

"Obviously someone does." The sick-hall attendant waited until I had settled Annique back onto the mattress. As I rose, she examined my face, and said quietly, "You mustn't worry, dear. We haven't lost a single child yet."

I followed her back downstairs to where the orphanage's only telephone rested in the side hall. I picked up the receiver and said hello.

The twang of an Indiana farmboy rang out loud and clear. "Well, hey there, Emily. That operator lady said she was pretty sure you'd be here. How you doing?"

"Fine," I said weakly. "How are you, Brad?"

"Oh, I'm just dandy. Reason I'm calling, the shipment of that gamma stuff is coming in before long. Thought you'd like to know."

I could not help but feel a little pang for the dark-haired girl lying upstairs. Why, oh why could it not have arrived earlier? But I put as much enthusiasm as I could into saying, "Oh, Brad, that's wonderful. I can't thank you all enough."

"Don't mention it. Got all the boys fired up, having something to think about besides just getting home." His cheery tone carried over the crackling line. "Hey, you won't believe what else has happened. After you were up here, I sent a letter back to the folks with one of the planes. Told them about the kids and how they'd been rounded up all over the place, no papers, can't hardly understand them. They called me last night."

My tone had drawn Rachel out from the kitchen. She stood staring at me, as I said, "From America?"

"Yeah, couldn't hardly believe it myself. Said it took 'em two solid days to get through. Anyway, they said they'd read my letter out in church. I was real embarrassed about that. I never did pay much attention to grammar and such. But they said that some of the church families were talking about maybe adopting a couple of the kids."

"That would be splendid," I cried, not trying to mask my excitement. "They are wonderful children, and they certainly could use a loving home."

"I'll write and tell 'em what you said. And that gamma stuff, it oughtta be here early next week, but we can't say for certain. There's some real rough weather over on the Continent, temperature's down to fifteen below in Belgium. They say it's headed this way."

After I hung up, Rachel said, "Well?"

"The temperature may be dropping again tonight."

"I am certain the excitement I just heard in your voice was not caused by a discussion of the weather," Rachel snapped. "Now what did the young man say?"

"The gamma globulin might be in soon," I announced, and explained about the weather.

"Thank God," Rachel breathed. "May this finally be the end to the illness."

"There's more," I said, and related the news about the adoptions.

Rachel grew very somber. "I wouldn't mention that just yet," she warned. "Not to anyone."

"Why on earth not?"

"Think of all the red tape we would have to unravel before that could actually happen. There is no need to get anyone's hopes up." She hesitated, then added, "If it happens at all. You don't know the Ministry like I do."

"What do they have to do with anything?"

"My dear, these children are officially under *their* care, not ours." Rachel's aged features creased into a worried frown. "I can't even begin to think how they might react to news that we are shipping their charges off to America."

"You're right," I agreed, but already my mind was racing. I lifted the receiver, and jiggled the handle until the operator came on the line.

Rachel demanded, "What are you doing?"

"Could you ask Fred to come pick me up, please?" I said to the operator. "Yes, that's right, I'm up at the orphanage."

Rachel watched me closely. "You're planning something."

"It's just an idea," I replied, already moving. "Do you know where they stored the stockings?"

IT IS VERY good that we cannot see into the future.

Had I known what we would soon face, I might have given up and said it was impossible, that I did not have the strength for the task and probably never would. But glimpses into the future are withheld from us, so I entered into my new work with the simple happiness of having something to fill my lonely days.

It was only much later, when the children had managed to learn English and the unseen crisis had finally been overcome, that I learned the meaning of the name Annique had given me.

Andiel was Czech for *angel*.

FOURTEEN

Since my visit with Mabel the travel agent, I had successfully avoided going anywhere in the village, except to church and my one trip to the fliers' pub. Sundays I slipped into the service at the very last moment, and left before the final hymn was sung. I took my meals either with Rachel or at the orphanage. I had avoided the High Street and the shops and the eyes. Until now.

I was so nervous that I didn't realize I had no idea where I was going until after Fred dropped me off and drove away. I waved and called his name, but the bulging gas bag blocked his rear vision. I dropped my hand, turned, and realized I had done the worst thing imaginable. I had called attention to myself. Faces up and down the street had turned my way. I ducked my head down into my collar, hugged the box of stockings up close to my chest, and started down the walk. I could feel the eyes following me.

"Oh, hello there, Miss Emily." The grocer's wife was a hefty woman, handsome in a work-worn way, with masses of tumbledown red hair. I had seen her several times, delivering loads of produce to the orphanage, but had never spoken with her before. Her red face was wreathed in smiles as she wiped her flour-covered hands on her spotted apron and stepped through the doorway. "How are you, dear?"

I was not sure I had heard correctly. *Dear*. "Fine, thank you," I faltered.

"Splendid day, now that it's stopped with the snow and all." The two of us blocked more than half the sidewalk.

People stepped around us, smiling and murmuring greetings. Not just to her either. To *us*. She pointed to the box in my arms. "What've you got there?"

"Oh, they're, ah, stockings."

Her eyes widened. "Ooooh, let us have a look, will you?"

"A-all right."

Eagerly she lifted the lid and pulled out one of the slender packages. She ran one finger under the cover, stroking the silk. "Ooh, that's nice, ain't it? Haven't had a pair of these since forty-two. Like to have broke my heart when they ran. My Danny, he took me to the picture show down Bottley way, back before the snows. Used my eyeliner and drawed up the back of my legs." She gave me a girlish grin. "Spent half the night pretending to check and make sure I had 'em on straight."

The friendliness of her welcome had warmed me to my toes. "Why don't you keep those?"

She used both hands to clasp the little cardboard container to her apron. "Oh, no, I couldn't possibly."

"Please, I want you to."

She clasped them even tighter. "Everybody in town knows how you came by these. Gotten people talking, it has, how you gave away the whole box to the orphanage."

I blushed at the thought of people having another reason to talk about me. "And who has given more to those children than you and your husband?"

"Well, but . . ." She eased the package out far enough to peek down at it. "Do you really think I should?"

"They're yours." To stave off further argument, I asked, "Do you know where I could find a camera?"

"Oh, I don't know if you can." She seemed genuinely apologetic over not being able to help. "All such as that is on the restricted list."

"I'm sorry, the what?"

"Means you can't buy it without a license. Couldn't have people going around taking pictures of what we didn't want the Jerries seeing, now, could we? 'Course, the war's over, but that doesn't mean the rules have been changed. Things move slow in this old land of ours." She pointed down the High Street. "Still, you could try the dry-goods shop down by the church."

As I started down the sidewalk, the woman added, "Pity about the news, isn't it?"

I turned back to ask her what news, but her husband called from within the shop. Hastily she headed for the door, tossing me a cheery, "Thanks ever so much for the lovely stockings, dear!"

I walked on down the High Street, carrying the smile with me. Clouds scuttled overhead, and the broad High Street was full of people hurrying after errands and home. Perhaps it was my imagination, but a couple of times I thought people nodded and murmured greetings in my direction. I kept my gaze fastened upon the scenery, for fear that if I looked down, I might find the curious and the gossip-hungry, and be sunk once more into gloom.

Arden was truly a lovely place. The High Street descended a gentle hill to join with the river and its ancient stone bridge. Its eleventh-century church rose beside the quietly flowing waters, the gray stone matching the river and the winter sky. The buildings on both sides dated back six and seven centuries, their beam-and-brick walls tilted and bowed by the weight of years. Lead-glass windows flowed like crystallized tears, turning the interiors into moving portraits of a bygone era.

But the town's pleasant air vanished the instant I stepped into the dry-goods store. The place was very full, its worn wooden floor scuffed by decades of farmers' boots. A trio of men in tweeds and trilby hats were examining shotguns, while their wives shook their heads over a bolt of heavy fabric laid upon the counter. As soon as I appeared in the doorway, all movement froze and all attention turned my way.

I felt my earlier nervousness return as the man behind the counter said, "Can I help you, Miss Robbins?"

Trying hard for a smile, I replied, "Perhaps. I hope so, Mr. . . ."

"Clyde Hoggin. My daughter helps out at the College." The wispy-haired storekeeper sniffed his disapproval. "What with all we've got going on and her mother being poorly, we'd be far better off if she spent less time with them kids and more seeing to my customers."

"We need all the help we can get," I pointed out, trying hard not to wilt under the sudden hostility.

"Not for long," muttered one of the men handling the guns.

"Aye, and it'll be a grand day when we see the last of that lot." The storekeeper walked down the counter toward me. "What can I do for you, then?"

"I need a camera and some film. A lot." That was as far as I got before what I had just heard settled in. "I'm sorry, what did you mean by seeing the last of the children?"

"Don't go spreading those rumors of yours," chided one of the women.

"It's not a rumor." The farmer was a barrel-chested man whose ruddy nose was mapped with blue veins. "I heard talk of it at the farmers' union this morning. Seems the Ministry's finally come to its senses."

"It'll be a sad day for Arden when the children are gone." The woman tilted her chin defiantly. "And it's people like you who give this town a bad name."

The man swelled indignantly. "Just because I'd rather keep my produce to feed my own lot, rather than toss it out to wastrels what nobody can even understand, that don't make me anything but smart."

"Hmph." The woman turned to me, and said quietly, "There's a rumor going around, dear, that the Ministry has decided to close down the orphanage."

"And I tell you," the man clamored, "that it ain't no rumor."

Storekeeper Hoggin stepped closer to where I was now

leaning heavily upon the counter. "We don't stock cameras, Miss. And you can't buy film without a permit." He pointed at the box under my arm. "What's there in the carton?"

"Stockings," I said, but my mind was held by the unbelievable news. "You mean, they want to take away our children?"

"Them ain't yours," the man in the corner snorted. "Nor the village's. They're nothing but a weight tied 'round all our ruddy necks."

"A carton of silk stockings?" The storekeeper's tone tightened with avarice. "Well now, in that case I imagine we can overlook such things as permits, can't we?"

The news was so shocking and spoken so harshly that I found myself grasping for something, anything to hold on to. "But nobody's said anything. Not even Reverend Albright."

"Aye, well, the vicar'll be round soon enough, I warrant." The thought gave the farmer a reason to smirk. "Him and his dicky heart."

The day's second shock struck me with the force of a blow. The wind was knocked out of me so that I could only manage a single word. "Heart?"

"The vicar doesn't like to talk about it," the woman said, moving up close as though to protect me from the farmer and his barrage of bad news. "Had rheumatic fever as a child, poor dear. Left him with a heart murmur."

"But he's always so active," I protested. "He never stops."

"Aye, that's his way of compensating, I suppose." The woman took my arm, which was very good, because I felt frozen to the spot. She guided me back outside. "You mustn't pay that lot in there any mind, dear. This happens to be a gathering place for the malcontents. I'd do my shopping elsewhere, if it didn't mean taking the bus to Bottley and back."

But I had no time for that. "Is it true what they were saying about the children?"

She sighed. "Rumors are as sure a product of war as sorrow. But this one has the stamp of truth, I'm afraid. It's come out of nowhere. I only heard about it an hour ago, but everyone seems to take it for granted that it's true."

"But it can't be—" At that moment I spotted Colin walking from the church doorway. "You'll have to excuse me," I said, and raced away.

Colin was climbing into the truck, but stopped at my approach. Even before I was close enough to speak, the grim expression to his face said it all. I felt something in my chest tear apart, as though a wound that had just begun to heal was violently reopened. "Oh, Colin. Isn't there anything we can do?"

"I'm going to the Ministry," he said tersely. "And I'm not leaving until I find out who's responsible."

Without another word I raced around and opened the passenger door. Tossing in the box of stockings, I clambered inside and declared, "Let's go."

MY SECOND JOURNEY to London was better than the first only because I was not so alone. Despite the steady flow of buses and lorries, there were very few automobiles. The broad streets seemed strangely empty, as though the city had been built for twice the traffic. The sidewalks were crowded, but people seemed as subdued as the city itself. I watched the faces wherever we stopped, especially when we approached one of the bomb sites. It seemed as though I was the only person who took any notice of the destruction.

We turned down a spacious avenue, and abruptly I found myself surrounded by the grandeur of the mighty British Empire. Tall buildings of white marble stood like solemn soldiers, flanked by pillars and statues and ranks of broad steps. When Colin pulled up in front of one of them, I asked, "Where are we?"

"Pall Mall."

I got out, but hesitated there by the truck. The buildings seemed so imposing, so utterly powerful and uncaring. It was only the sight of Colin, poor tired Colin tromping up that expanse of grand white stairs all alone, that gave me the strength to go forward.

We passed through a pair of enormous bronze doors. I read a placard beside one that said the doors had been made from cannons melted down after some battle. The interior was no less dignified, with a vast circular chandelier suspended from a ceiling thirty feet high. I stayed close to Colin as we crossed the marble-tiled floor, feeling very, very small.

The gray-haired man guarding the entrance barrier wore row after row of ribbons and medals on his ancient uniform. He gave us an impassive stare. "Yes?"

"Displaced persons," Colin said, his voice clipped by tension and worry.

"Second floor, down the hall on your left. Take the stairs there."

Upstairs the building was much less imperial, full of bustling offices and hurrying people and uniforms and voices. Nobody paid us the least attention. I sat on a hard wooden bench while Colin went in to announce our arrival and, as he put it, demand a meeting with someone who could do something about this mess.

As I sat and waited, I found myself growing increasingly aware of my appearance. The clothes had seemed fine when I put them on this morning, as I had planned to go no farther afield than the orphanage. But within the walls of this stuffy Ministry, I realized that I looked a mess.

My shoes were scuffed and worn. The hem of my skirt was muddy from a walk through the orphanage garden the afternoon before. One of the infants had also stained my lapel with formula. I wore no makeup. My hair was pinned haphazardly into place. My hands were chapped raw from scrubbing floors.

The meeting was a misery from beginning to end. It was the only time I had ever seen Colin lose his temper. The woman was precise and prune-faced, with her hair in a bun so tight it drew her eyes into slits. She wore a tailored gray suit, and cast a disapproving eye over my appearance. I found myself so intimidated I was afraid to open my mouth.

Colin grew red-faced and bitter when he learned the Ministry could not even tell us where the children were going, or when. His anger seemed to please the woman to no end. Her name was Miss Hillary Tartish, and she watched Colin storm and protest with amused contempt. "The children are not your concern, Reverend, ah . . ."

"Albright," Colin snapped.

"Of course. The children are the Ministry's responsibility, to do with as the Ministry sees fit." Her gaze was as severe as her dress. "A fact that seems to have escaped your attention for far too long."

"Those children are alive because we looked after them," Colin flashed angrily. "And not a lick of help or thanks did we receive from your lot."

"What you fail to recognize, Reverend," Miss Tartish responded glacially, "is that it is precisely because of your meddlesome ways that our own carefully planned and logical routine was so thoroughly disrupted."

"The children still needed food," Colin barked. "They still needed clothes. What kept you from sending supplies when we were so desperately short?"

"Those very same shortages are exactly why we shall all be better off distributing those children around the other displaced persons camps. Facilities, I might add, which are *much* better run than your own."

What she had just said struck me with the force of a slap to my face. "A *camp*? You're sending these children to a camp full of adults?"

"Full of displaced persons," she replied icily. "Which is *precisely* what these young people are, in case that has slipped your notice."

"They're not," I cried. "They're *children*. They've been horribly scarred by war and their experiences, and they need love and care. Not to be lost in the mass of humanity in a camp!"

"I've heard quite enough of this nonsense," she snapped. "For your information, Europe is positively awash with these displaced persons. There is neither the time nor the resources to give them special treatment of *any* sort." She looked down her nose with frigid contempt. "Your lot has done nothing but set a bad example, and upset our carefully prepared plans."

I turned to Colin. "This is absurd."

"What this is, young lady, is official government policy." Her words were a biting lash. "We shall begin transferring those children by the beginning of next month, and close you down entirely three weeks later!"

"We'll see about that," Colin cried, rising to his feet.

"Yes," Miss Tartish retorted, remaining seated behind her vast empty desk. "Yes, we certainly shall."

It was only when we were back in the truck that Colin dropped his head to the steering wheel and moaned, "I made an absolute shambles of that."

"No, you didn't," I protested, as worried at that point for Colin as I was for the children. "You did everything you could."

"Which was nothing at all." He turned hopeless eyes toward me. "What on earth am I going to tell the others?"

The drive back began in a silence more dismal than the one that had accompanied us in. I wanted to ask him about his heart, but Colin was already so despondent that I did not dare. Instead, I tried to force away the quiet by talking about Brad's telephone call and my trip into the village.

"I'm not surprised he wanted your stockings," Colin said when I was finished. "Clyde Hoggin has made a small fortune as a spiv."

"A what?"

"A spiv is someone who deals on the black market. There's such as that in every town." Colin shook his head. "His daughter Hannah is one of the quiet ones, and no wonder, given her father's nature. Whenever she can manage she helps out in the sick-hall." He tried to offer me a smile. "It's a pity God doesn't operate heaven on a family plan, for I fear that's the only way her father will ever see the eternal city."

The sadness in his eyes threatened to break my heart. "I'm so sorry, Colin."

"And you are a dear to be so concerned for our little woes." He drove on in silence for a while, before offering, "I used to be a fair hand at taking photographs."

"You did?"

"I even apprenticed to a portrait maker, back before I received my calling." He gave his chin a thoughtful rub. "It's not such a bad idea you've had, Emily. Jolly nice, in fact. We could send a few pictures over to Brad's church, and save the others for ourselves. You know, in case—"

"Take the stockings and buy all the film you can," I cried, cutting him off. I could not bear to hear him say that our little charges might be taken away, lost in a maelstrom of

Ministry papers. Or that the photographs might someday become our only link to what once had been. The thought of not even knowing where they might land cut like a knife. I could not hear him speak the words.

FIFTEEN

The next morning Rachel decided to take our protest up with the Arden village council. Fred was busy with an out-of-town call, so I took the bus up the hill to the orphanage. I was no longer afraid of being seen and stared at and whispered over. I could not explain why going to the Ministry had affected me in that way. Or perhaps it was the way the grocer's wife had greeted me. Or the avaricious shopkeeper, more concerned with my stockings than with my needs or our children. Yes, I thought. *Our* children. I was far too busy worrying over where they might end up, and under whose care, to be concerned with the murmured conversations and the looks shot my way. Even if some of the half-heard words were meant as arrows, I kept my head held high.

The bus was an ancient round-shouldered affair that wheezed and rattled at each stop, and belched great clouds of black smoke as it started off again. I sat and stared out the rain-streaked window, and found myself thinking of the river, and of Rachel's words from the day before. How I needed to hold on to silence in order to hear the Lord's quiet voice. The more I came to know that tall stately woman, the more I admired her. My thoughts about Rachel and the river pushed aside my worries, and left no room for the snide conversations swirling about me. Instead, I was held by an image of the river, the rain falling softly upon the surface, the steady current flowing on undisturbed.

The rivulets of thought seemed to run together in my mind. The village, the people seated about me, the children, my own troubles—a world full of woes and hurts and misgivings. All the while, currents of love and healing ran deep and unseen, but we could only see the rain marring the surface.

The bus pulled up in front of the orphanage's gates. As I walked down the long lane I struggled to focus, though a single image remained to tug at me. The river flowed on, steady and ceaseless, waiting for me to reach down and draw from its eternal strength.

THE MOOD AT the orphanage was morose, and worsened steadily with the day and the weather. By midafternoon it had turned so cold the rain began freezing as it fell. Icicles grew from windows and eaves and tree limbs. There was no hope of the nighttime volunteers arriving. Even walking down the front stairs meant risking a broken limb.

After the dinner dishes were cleaned, I sat with Annique until sleep stole her away. The doctors were increasingly certain we faced a bout of hepatitis; that particular strain, though serious, was almost never life-threatening in children. I sat there on the side of her bed and watched her sleeping face. She was a remarkable pixie, a child's face stamped with such womanly features, honed far beyond her years by experiences I could scarcely imagine. She and all these other slumbering forms had come to mean so much to me. I could scarcely bear the thought of their being taken and split apart and sent goodness knew where.

Eventually I went back downstairs and found Rachel standing at the back French doors. Without asking, I made two cups of tea, and went over to join her. Her smile at my approach was tinted by the same sadness that filled my heart.

"How sweet of you, my dear," she said, accepting the cup and then opening the door. "Come, let us get a breath of air."

We stepped carefully onto the grand back veranda. The patio was all slate tile and marble inlay, with Grecian urns decorating the stone wall. In order to avoid the subject on everyone's mind, I asked her whom the house belonged to.

"Nobody. Or rather, the National Trust, an organization founded some time ago to look after properties such as these, when a family either dies out or loses its fortune. Such properties then become a part of our national heritage."

"Or war colleges. Or orphanages."

"Precisely." Her breath smoked as she examined me over the rim of her cup. "You have changed, my dear."

I stared up at the night sky. The clouds had vanished, and the air was scrubbed clean by the rain. I had never seen so many stars. I could feel her eyes upon me, but did not lower my gaze. Imprinted there upon the star-flecked skies were fleeting images of all the past few days had held. Yet I found it difficult to put any of it into words. Finally I said, "The river spoke to me."

"Ah." Rachel's voice altered, and I realized she had turned her face toward the heavens. "It is remarkable how God will teach us through the silent things, is it not?"

I nodded, though I knew she could not see me. "Almost as though the hard times open us to lessons we would otherwise prefer not to notice."

"What a glorious thought." She patted my arm. "I will bid you good night, my dear. Rest well."

I stayed on the veranda as long as I could. The stars became friends that night, and the silhouette of the big silent house, and the dark images of trees sleeping in the cold air. When I finally allowed the cold to drive me back inside, I knew I would hold that image close to my heart for the rest of my days. Despite the present sadness, despite all in my life that was not as I might have wished, still the Lord was with me. That I knew for certain.

IT WAS THE quietest dawn I had ever known. This was not the silence of falling snow, with sweet whispers of wind and flakes. Instead, the world was held in a frozen grip, breathless and awestruck by nature's quiet power.

I rose from my bed in the large room off the kitchen which we were using as a pantry. There was no stirring from the other four mattresses spread upon the stone floor. Quietly I slipped into my clothes. Despite the stove that we had kept burning all night long, I could see my breath. Shivering and rubbing my arms, I carefully stepped onto the back veranda.

The sun had not appeared over the horizon. The eastern sky was rimmed with gold, yet overhead the stars seemed so bright and close I could almost touch them. The ground was white and layered with a drifting blanket of fog. The trees, the veranda's stone railing, the house, everything was enveloped in frost. Icicles dripped like winter's fingers.

As the sun rose, the clear crystals were transformed into prisms of gold and orange and red. The field stretching out before me became a giant mirror, reflecting the sky's glorious colors.

That morning, I was assigned to the sick-hall to assist with breakfast. Annique sat up in bed, too weak to do much walking, yet wanting to follow me with her eyes. Each passage up and down the central aisle, I would pause long enough to smile or speak a few words she could not understand. Her open dark-eyed gaze warmed me.

"Emily. Oh, there you are." I rose from gathering the breakfast bowls to find Rachel hurrying toward me. Her cane made sharp thunks on the wooden floor, marking time and her passage. "Did you ask Colin to make photographs of the children?"

I was uncertain how to respond. "It was just an idea. I'm sorry, perhaps I should have asked—"

"Oh, don't be silly. If Colin thinks it is acceptable, who am I to object? Or anyone else, for that matter." She waved her hand. "Never mind that. He's downstairs waiting for you."

"Now?" I stared out the window at the utterly frozen world. "How did he get here?"

Rachel's gaze joined mine by the frost-covered window. "By horseback."

"I HAD A friend who was coming up this way with an empty cart," Colin explained, hauling equipment into the parlor we used as a playroom. "He was only too glad for the company."

I could not begin to tell him how happy I was to see him and his smile. His presence seemed to light up the orphanage in a way the brilliant sunshine had failed to do, dispelling all the gloom wherever he went. "But don't you need to be working with the Ministry?"

"Abler hands than mine have taken that on." He opened a strapped wooden crate and extracted a collapsible tripod. "The mayor is personally seeing if any of his contacts in Whitehall can help us out."

The children did not know what to make of Colin's equipment. They clustered toward the back of the room, watching Colin with solemn eyes. We were tremendously short-staffed, what with the roads turned to slick ribbons of ice. I stopped in every now and then and saw the changes take place in fleeting segments. On one trip between the laundry and the bedrooms, my hands full of freshly starched sheets, I saw that a few of the bolder lads had moved up close. They watched intently as Colin wrestled with equipment that had not been touched since before the war. Another trip, and I realized they were watching his face far more than his hands, studying with the intensity of those who had survived through constant caution.

Having their pictures taken awoke some dormant memory within many of the children. It did not matter that they were friends with Colin. Something about the big apparatus and the lights and the need to stand there alone terrified them.

Rachel walked in and inspected the frightened face standing before the camera, and the equally alarmed ones waiting their turn. Impatiently she declared, "This will simply not do. Not at all."

"They're not going to make a very appealing impression," Colin agreed. "Not to mention the fact that most of the younger ones have vanished."

Rachel turned to me and demanded, "Well, what are you going to do about this?"

"Me?"

"It's your idea." She swept out one long arm. "Something must be done to make the children come alive."

All the children who had not run off were watching me. Perhaps three dozen little faces, looking up to me in silent appeal. "For starters, let's turn off the lamp," I decided.

"We'll be fighting shadows if we do," Colin warned.

"Well, Rachel's right. We're just wasting film the way things are now."

Thoughtfully, Colin moved to the big bay window at the parlor's far end. He stood there a moment, studying the window and the sky, then turned back to me and said, "Sit down here on the window seat, would you?"

I saw what he had in mind. "Oh no, I couldn't."

"Why not?"

I tried to push my hair into some kind of order. "I don't have a touch of makeup."

Colin laughed. The sound rang through the high-ceilinged chamber. "Don't be daft. We're after the children. And besides, you look marvelous."

Reluctantly I allowed him to place me so the sunlight fell directly upon my face. The memory of that one laugh seemed to echo about the room.

The sunlight was bright enough so that one of the lamps could be turned off. The other was stationed in the far corner. When I was comfortable, he led one of the children over to me. It seemed almost natural for the child to climb up into my lap. I noticed she was staring at the locket I wore around my neck, so I slid it off. I helped the little fingers pry open the clasp.

When I realized what was inside, I could not hold back a little gasp of surprise.

"What's the matter?"

"Nothing." And I was surprised a second time to discover that what I had said was the truth.

The locket was a little golden heart, with Grant's picture embedded in one half, and my own in the other. I had forgotten his picture was there. I sat there in the sunlight, wondering at the events of the past few weeks, and the ability of my own heart to heal such that I would even forget I still carried his picture.

Colin finally spoke up again. "That's it."

I looked up, squinting into the light. "What?"

"We're done with this one, let's move on."

I allowed the child to slide down, and held out my arms for the next one. The locket and chain still dangled from my hand. When the boy was settled, he sat and watched as I pulled Grant's picture free. The camera's click was almost imperceptible. A moment later, the boy was replaced by a shy little girl. I heard Colin ask, "Can you make her look up?"

"I'll try." The girl watched wide-eyed as I set aside the locket, then took Grant's picture and tore it in two. Then put the pieces together and tore them again. A third time, then I lifted one hand, and let the little pieces fall to the floor. In the sunlight, they looked like tiny dry snowflakes, and the girl in my lap laughed out loud.

Colin clicked the camera, then declared, "Perfect. Absolutely spot-on."

I heard the excitement in his voice, and hugged the girl before letting her go. This time, the next child did not need to be led over. And the time after, there was a little tussle between two who wanted to be next. I could not see much beyond the sunlight streaming through the window, but I heard quiet movements through the chamber's far end. Next came three children, in descending order from an overly thin nine or ten year old to a toddler. But they all shared the same slanted dark eyes. They stood before me, holding hands, solemnly looking up as I asked, "Should we do these together?"

"I would think so," came a woman's reply. "They're sisters, as far as we can tell."

"Is that you, Rachel?"

"Yes. Your lunch is growing cold."

"We shouldn't stop," Colin announced. "The light is perfect."

So we stayed where we were, photographing one child after another, allowing those who we knew were siblings to sit together. Some refused to look up, some peeked shyly from the protection of my arms. A few smiled. Most took it calmly, once they saw that I was there with them, content to sit and play with my locket. My arms grew tired, my legs numb. But my smile seemed to strengthen with the passing hours.

BY THE TIME we finished for the day, Colin was too tired to journey home. Which was just as well, since the world outside our orphanage remained locked in a solid sheet of ice. Food had arrived in the form of four cart-loads of produce, and after dinner those of us who were not on duty sat around the scarred kitchen worktable. We were a glum little group, unwilling to say much for all were caught by the same worries, and the same lack of answers. To look into one another's face was enough to know that all hearts were wrenched by fears for our children's fates.

The next morning we started off bright and early. It was good to be busy with work like this, as it kept our minds too active for more than an occasional pang. Many of the children had accepted the pictures as a part of the normal routine, though some still had to be coaxed.

Toward lunchtime I heard Rachel call my name. I could not move for the child in my lap, so I replied with, "In here!"

The lamp kept me from seeing more than a silhouette step through the door. "How are things going?"

"Fine," Colin said, his voice tinged with fatigue, "so long as our Emily sits and holds them."

"You really must rest, Colin. That is, unless you're intent upon working yourself into an early grave."

"Don't even think such a thing," I pleaded.

The pair turned my way, I could see their shadows shift behind the lamp. For some reason, the quiet inspection made me uncomfortable. I asked, "Are we done with this one?"

"Not quite." Colin moved back to the camera, and I heard it click. "All right, let's be having the next one."

"You realize, of course," Rachel pointed out, "that we shall be having three hundred pictures of our dear Emily along with the children."

"Not necessarily a bad thing," Colin murmured. Then more loudly, "We've got quite a number who still don't want to come down. They're afraid. And we haven't even started with those in the sick-hall."

"But why . . ." Rachel's voice faded as a drumming sound began to fill the chamber. "What is that noise?"

There was a moment's silence before Colin said slowly, "I know what it sounds like. But that can't be."

We all moved toward the window and stood there squinting upward and trying to make out a tiny black speck against the sun's glare. The drumming noise grew steadily louder, until Colin finally declared, "That's a helicopter, and the bloke's coming in for a landing."

"What," Rachel cried. "Here?"

"Out the back!" Colin shouted, and sprinted for the door. He was followed by a herd of children, few of whom understood exactly what was going on. But the commotion was enough to draw out everyone who was well enough to walk.

Together we raced down the back hall and out through the glass double doors. The veranda had lost its slippery covering, but the house still stood in an icy wonderland that sparkled beneath the brilliant sun.

Though blocked from view by the manor, the helicopter was much louder out here. We stood and shielded our eyes, when suddenly its black and ungainly form came roaring overhead. The children shrieked and either clung to the nearest adult or fled back indoors.

I had seen pictures of these machines, but had never been close to one before. The wind beat at me with appalling force. The noise was worse than anything I could have imagined, even when it passed overhead and continued toward the frozen lawn. I was very frightened. I did not see how that ugly, lumbering metal beast could possibly remain airborne. I might very well have fled inside myself, but I was held in place by a dozen pairs of frantic arms.

Then I spotted a friendly red-haired figure waving at me through the helicopter's open side door, and I felt a flood of both relief and excitement. The drumming rotors began to slow, and the noise dropped first to an angry whine and then to silence. Bob jumped from the doorway and called, "Hey there, Emily! What do you think of my new jalopy?"

"Ugly and noisy!" Gently I coaxed the anxious arms and fingers free, and pried myself loose from the clustering children. A few of the braver ones moved with me, clutching my skirt and hiding behind me. "What on earth are you doing here?"

Bob kept bent over as he walked out from beneath the still-swinging rotors. "Stuff came in yesterday before the freeze shut us down. We been waiting for the roads to clear, but it's supposed to get colder again tonight. The chopper's here to take the doctor back to Norfolk, he's on duty."

"Chopper?" Colin moved up beside me. "Doctor?"

"Hey, Reverend. How you been?"

"Fine. Cold." Colin shook the American's hand. "Did you say you had a doctor on board?"

I noticed Bob's face, and interrupted with, "What happened to your eye?"

"Oh. That." Sheepishly Bob touched the shiner. "My last trip took me by way of Berlin. Ran into Grant Rockwell at the Officers' Club."

"Oh, Bob. You didn't."

"Couldn't help but tell him what I thought of what he'd done," he continued doggedly.

"Yes, you most certainly could have," I protested.

"Maybe so," shouted Bradley Atwater, as he hustled under the rotors and trotted over. "But it shore must've been a sight, seeing Grant stretched out on his back like that."

I stared at the two of them. "You knocked Grant out?"

"Guess maybe I did at that," Bob mumbled, studying the ground at his feet.

I worked my mouth open and closed a few times, then managed, "Bob McIntyre, I don't know whether to slap you or hug you."

"I don't recall," Colin Albright said, not trying to mask his grin, "anything in the Good Book about our having such a choice."

"If you're gonna take a swing, do it to this side," Bob said, pointing to his uninjured cheek. "The other one's still kind of sore."

I let the laugh escape then, and reached out to take them both in a hug. "I can't believe you're here."

"Thank the chopper," Brad said, flashing his brilliant grin. "That there's the dangdest thing I ever did see."

Another figure descended from the helicopter's door, this one moving awkwardly. He shouted over, "Is it safe to come out now?"

"That's the doc," Brad said, waving the guy toward us. "Ain't half bad, for a navy feller. But he's never been more'n two feet off the ground before. Spent the whole trip moaning like a lovesick calf."

"That's where we found the gamma globulin," Bob offered, glad to have the attention turn from his face. "At the American naval base in Norfolk. When we went over to pick it up, the doc here heard about what we were doing and insisted on coming along."

"Didn't tell him nothing about the chopper till he had

signed on," Brad declared proudly. "Figured we might have a little trouble with that one."

At closer inspection, the doctor did have a decidedly greenish tint. But he gave us a little salute and stood as straight as he could manage. "Dr. Donald Taft," he said weakly. "Where are the sick children?"

SIXTEEN

Doctor Taft gave the first two children a cursory inspection, then declared flatly, "Infectious hepatitis. No question."

Rachel was unsure how to take this abrupt young man in his flashy naval uniform. "But you haven't seen the others."

"No need." Even so, he moved to the next bed, inspected tongue and eyes and felt for the lymph nodes, then flipped back the blanket and kneaded the belly just below the rib cage. Then he looked up at Rachel. "I've seen enough of these cases to know them in my sleep. Boats are perfect breeding grounds for hepatitis. You'll notice the jaundiced eyes, the swollen livers, the physical apathy. How many cases are there?"

"One hundred and eight," Rachel replied instantly. Another two had come down the day before, and three had been recently released.

"A hundred children?" He took in the chamber with an impatient sweep of his arm. "You mean to tell me that all of these children are down with the same ailment?"

A warning light glimmered in Rachel's eyes. "That is correct."

The doctor looked positively incensed. "Then why in heaven's name have you waited so long to inoculate them?"

She drew herself up, and brandished her cane in the doctor's face. "Because we haven't had any choice!"

The children did not like this tone at all. Frightened wails rose from several of the nearby beds. Rachel flashed a furious glance at the doctor, then moved off to help the other women soothe them. I stepped forward and said quietly, "We've been trying to get the doses for over a month, ever since the local doctors finally decided it was most likely hepatitis."

"There shouldn't have been any question from the beginning, " the doctor huffed.

"The Ministry has dragged its feet over everything," Colin Albright said, moving up beside me. "Plus there are shortages of almost all medicines. I suppose they think there are other cases more urgent than these children."

"Not in my book," he said, rising to his feet. "All right, let's get started."

But it was not that simple. The children remained tense and skittish, as they were toward everything new. Years of survival had honed their apprehension toward anything out of the ordinary. They hid themselves, peeking out, racing away whenever we came to gather them together. It did not help that the friction between Rachel and the doctor was evident to all who saw them together.

The change began the instant it finally sank in to the Americans that we could not communicate with the children.

The implications of this hit with such force that the doctor stopped in the front hallway, an expression of utter bewilderment on his face, as he watched Colin coax out a pair of little girls from the front hall's broom closet. He did so with gentle tones and kind eyes, since the words meant nothing.

Slowly the doctor turned to where Rachel was standing defiantly upon the bottom stair. "You haven't had any help at all," he said quietly. "Have you?"

"From the Ministry?" She humphed. "A great heaping lot of misery and very little else."

"All right," Colin said, walking over, his arms full of a young girl who clutched tightly to his neck. "I suppose we can start with this one."

"No, not like this. It won't do," the doctor said absently. Then to Rachel, "I owe you an apology."

"Yes," she replied, still working on her head of steam. "You certainly do."

"I had no idea." He turned back to where I was standing beside Colin and Bob. He rubbed his chin thoughtfully. "If this is going to work, we need to do it in an orderly fashion."

"Not a hope," the American pilot declared. "These kids are spooked."

"I don't know about that," Brad countered, moving up behind us. He asked Bob, "You pack those boxes of chocolate like I told you?"

"All we had room for."

"Chocolate?" Colin's eyes lit up. "You have chocolate?"

"Six boxes' worth of Hershey's," Bob confirmed.

"What we need," Brad said, "is for a few of the kids who are leaders to come out and get the goodies. We can give them the shots while their minds are occupied."

"Make a game of it," Colin said. "Splendid idea."

"I know just the one to start with," I said. "Can one of you gentlemen help me?"

In the end, it was Colin who came upstairs with me. I chose him because the children already knew him. We walked down the sickroom hall to where Annique lay in her little bed. As soon as she was certain that I was coming to her, she raised her arms and cried out, "Andiel Emily!" It was the same thing she said every time I approached.

I accepted her embrace, then showed in sign language that I wanted Colin to lift her up. She made no objection, but she did not let go of my hand for an instant.

Together the three of us made our way back downstairs.

It was a little awkward, but I stayed close so that Annique could both keep hold of my hand and watch me with her solemn-eyed gaze from her place on Colin's chest. Those children who saw our little procession eased up, releasing a bit of their tension, and followed a few steps behind us.

We moved into the back hallway, where the doctor was using a long trestle table as his stall. Hastily he had spread a clean white sheet on it, and was showing Bob how to prepare the syringes and needles and vials of gamma globulin. The pilot's movements were awkward in his long rubber gloves.

Rachel sat at the table's end, paper and pencil ready to note the children as they were inoculated. Brad was busy bringing in boxes and stacking them by the back door. Sunlight streamed through the tall glass doors, glinting upon the two metal sterilizers set up behind the table. One of the autoclave doors was open, revealing a further pile of needles and glass syringes.

"We'll show them everything right out front," the doctor decided. "Let them see we are hiding nothing at all."

Colin demanded, "Are you going to inoculate the sick ones as well?"

"Can't hurt, long as we have enough to go around. In any case I had planned to give them an injection of vitamins." He spun about, searching among the unopened boxes. "What did we do with the Hershey's?"

"Right here," Bob said, reaching down and coming up with an armful of the black-and-silver slabs.

Colin watched with round eyes as the candy spilled onto the table. "Not in my wildest dreams have I imagined so much chocolate in one place."

"Take that scalpel and start cutting them in two," the doctor ordered. "We need to make sure there's enough to go around."

With my free hand, I accepted the first half and clumsily unwrapped the candy. Then I offered it to Annique. She hesitated a moment, until she caught the first whiff. I could see it happen, because her nostrils flared, and her eyes flew open wide. Timidly she accepted the black slab, and took a tiny bite. Then she whispered a question, as though she could not believe what she was tasting. *"Chokolada?"*

"It's for you," I said, smiling at her astonishment.

She looked up at where a half-dozen little faces were peering through the stair railing. *"Chokolada!"* she cried, taking another bite. She raised the bar over her head and shrilled again, *"Chokolada!"*

The cry was taken up by a myriad of high-pitched voices up and down the length of the house. Overhead we heard the quick scurrying of feet.

"This is one for the books," Bob declared.

The doctor lifted up a syringe, holding it directly in front of Annique's face. Solemnly she watched him, and me, and the syringe. But she did not move, not even when the spot on her arm was swabbed with alcohol, and the needle was inserted. She winced, but did not cry out as the plunger was pushed and the needle removed. With my free hand I stroked her face and whispered, "I'm so proud of you I could burst."

Annique rewarded me with her first smile since she had become ill. She took another bite, watched as the doctor fitted a Band-Aid on her arm, then gave me another smile and cooed, *"Chokolada."*

"Okay," the doctor said, "let's try another one."

SEVENTEEN

When Marissa awoke, the bedside clock's illuminated dial read just after midnight. In the far corner, Gran was turned away from her and breathing softly. As quietly as she could, she slid from her bed. Carrying her robe in one hand and her slippers in the other, she tiptoed from the room and closed the door behind her.

The entire house seemed illuminated, softly glowing with the same warm light that filled her mind and heart. For several days now, she had wanted to do something for Gran. Something special, something that would show in more than words how grateful Marissa was for Gran sharing her story.

The times of sitting and listening to her grandmother had taken on a timeless air, as though she was lifted beyond herself and her illness. Not even the concerns of her outside world could touch her then, neither the worries she had about growing up, nor how she looked, nor how things were at school, nor if her friends really liked her, nor if she would ever grow into someone even halfway beautiful. None of that mattered while her grandmother spoke. Not even that she had been denied her dream of traveling to Hawaii. Not even that.

During their times of sharing, Marissa was free, truly

able to expand beyond herself. It was an astonishing discovery, the first time she could ever remember something like that happening. Her grandmother's open honesty was showing her not just a new place and time, but an entirely new way of looking at the world.

Her grandmother's words were reshaping even the way she saw herself. As though everything was being brought into a sharper, better focus. As though she was really growing up. And Marissa wanted to do something to thank Gran for this incredible gift.

She waited until she was downstairs before she slipped on her robe and turned on a light. She entered the kitchen, opened the drawer beside the phone, and pulled out Gran's personal telephone book. Try as she might, she could not remember their last name. Only that it was something unpronounceable.

Page by page, she ran her finger down the names. The closer she came to the end, the more she feared that she had somehow missed them. Which would mean trying to move the conversation around so that she could get the name from Gran. That would be very risky, for her grandmother was too sharp to be easily fooled. If she suspected something, she would demand to know what Marissa had in mind. And Marissa knew she could not lie to her grandmother. Even if telling the truth meant having Gran order her to forget the idea and not mention it again.

The book was very hard to read, especially where the names and numbers had been penciled in years ago, then erased and the addresses changed time after time.

Marissa's eyes began burning from the effort of reading her grandmother's jerky scrawl. Then her finger stopped, and her eyes opened wide. There it was. Hank and Annique Rygalchyk. She lifted the telephone receiver and dialed the number.

When a sleepy voice answered, she said, "Uncle Hank? I don't know if you remember me, but this is Marissa. I'm Gran's, I mean Emily's granddaughter." The voice on the other end came to instant alert.

Marissa responded with, "No sir, she's fine. And I'm better. Really. That was why I was calling. I'm sorry it's so late, but I needed to wait until Gran was asleep. Is Aunt Annique there?"

A moment's pause, then a softly accented voice came on the phone. Marissa had to take a long breath, because all the stories Gran had been telling suddenly pulled tightly together. The years and the distance dividing her from them had abruptly disappeared. "Aunt Annique? This is Marissa. Yes ma'am, I'm a whole lot better. Really. But that's not why I'm calling. Gran has been telling me about, well, stories when you were younger." Another long breath, then, "And I've had this idea."

GRAN'S SLEEPY VOICE greeted her with, "Did I just hear your voice, dear?"

"I talked with Daddy and George." Which was true. She had called them after she talked with Aunt Annique. "Buddy is off somewhere with Momma."

"You were on the phone a long time."

Marissa glanced at the clock. It was twenty minutes to one. She had only spoken to her family for ten minutes. But there had been a lot to discuss with Annique. A whole lot. "I'll call collect next time."

"Don't be silly. It's two days till Christmas, and your family is on the other side of the world. Call them as much as you like." Gran rolled over and sat up. "How is everyone?"

"Fine. They told me to give you a hug and wish you Merry Christmas again."

"Thank you." A smile flitted across Gran's features. "Would you just take a look at yourself?"

Marissa was seated with her legs dangling over the side of the bed, bouncing up and down. "I'm feeling a whole lot better, Gran."

"Yes, so I notice. You mustn't push yourself too hard, mind. We don't want you suffering a relapse." She stood and slipped on a robe. "I suppose you'll be wanting another midnight cup of cocoa."

"And some more of the story," Marissa added, far too excited to sleep. She slipped from her bed and followed her grandmother from the room. "I can't wait to find out what happens next."

GRAN'S STORY

It froze again that night. But we did not have time to notice. We continued with the inoculations until all of us were stumbling with fatigue. The more tired the children became, the easier it was to handle them. We did not stop until well after midnight, and then we collapsed in exhausted heaps. Soon after dawn we were up and running once more.

By now, the children had accepted the men and the picture-taking and the shots. I was no longer required to sit and hold the younger ones. So I positioned them, Colin took their pictures, then they were hustled back for an injection and a chocolate.

As soon as the sun melted away the worst of the frost, some of the other children went out to clamber around the helicopter. Just after lunch, we finished off the serum while injecting the last children in the sick-hall. There was more chocolate to go around, which created a near riot when the children realized we were giving out seconds. Then it was time to see off the three Americans. It felt as though we were saying farewell to lifelong friends. Even Rachel, exhausted as she was, unwound enough to give the doctor a long hug.

It was as I walked the trio back to the helicopter that Bradley mentioned, "Seems like something more than sick kids is bothering you folks."

I tried for a smile. "Is it that obvious?"

"Folks gathering in corners for a quiet sigh when they should be happy," Bob offered. "That's pretty noticeable."

"You've been so kind," I replied. "We didn't want to involve you with our problems."

"Hey." With a grand sweep of his arm, Bradley took in the chopper and the doctor and the orphanage. "In case you haven't noticed, we're already involved."

So I told them about the difficulties we had faced since the beginning with the Ministry. Then I described the present threat of closure. The trio of faces grew steadily grimmer as I recounted the meeting with Miss Hillary Tartish, and her plans for our children.

Brad's tone was taut as a whip. "So they're gonna farm out these kids to a load of camps?"

"Over my dead body," Bob muttered.

"We're doing everything we can," Colin interjected, stepping up beside me. "The village authorities have spent the past two days desperately seeking someone with sufficient clout to halt this madness."

"Madness is right." Brad rubbed a tired hand over his crew cut. "You said you got them to back off before, why not now?"

"Because we threatened to hold up their misdeeds to the light of day," Colin replied. "Unfortunately, closing an orphanage and moving the children elsewhere does not interest our press."

The three Americans carried their grim expressions into the helicopter. As Bob settled behind the pilot's controls, Brad leaned through the open door and said, "It ain't right, Miss Emily."

"I'm sorry you had to hear about it." I tried hard to reward them with a smile. "No matter what happens from here on out, today you boys are heroes."

"I don't feel like a hero," Brad replied as overhead the rotors chuffed through their first rotation. "I feel like calling out the cavalry."

WE STOOD ON the back veranda, too weary to do more than wave and smile as the helicopter lifted up. Three American faces could be seen in the sun-glinted windows, waving and reflecting the same tiredness we felt.

After the noise and the wind had vanished with the chopper, Colin and I stood there in quiet satisfaction. The sun was directly overhead, blazing down from a cloudless sky, warming us despite the day's lingering chill. I closed my eyes and lifted my face upward, wishing there were some way to open up and drink the sunlight in like water.

"I don't know when I have felt so tired," Colin confessed.

That brought me around. "That's the first time I've ever heard you admit to any weakness."

"I have so many," he admitted quietly, "I hate to talk about them."

"Like your heart," I said, and was instantly contrite. "I'm sorry, Colin. I shouldn't have said that."

"It's all right. I suppose it had to come out sometime." He raised his hand. "Only don't start about needing to take it easy. Please, not that."

"But you do."

"The entire free world has been called to give until it hurts," he replied. "That is one of the tragedies of war. Why should I do any less?"

Before I could think of a reply, Rachel came racing back outside. "Hurry up, both of you. Fred's just come through the front gates. He's done the rounds and is bringing in replacements."

She vanished, but still we did not move, as though we were both held by something unfinished. Colin cleared his throat, then asked, "Emily, would you perhaps care to join me for a meal tomorrow evening?"

"I would be honored," I replied shyly, retreating behind the same odd formality I heard in his voice.

"There's not much on offer these days, I'm afraid. But we could walk down to the pub and see what they have on the board."

It felt as though the sun reached down and generated a warmth inside me. "I'm sure it will be just fine."

THE ONLY REASON I knew I made it upstairs before conking out was because I woke up in my bed. My clothes were scattered in a haphazard line down the hall and into the bedroom. I dressed as I retraced my steps, stopping in the kitchen for a cup of tea and two slices of stale bread with margarine—it was all I had in my larder, and I did not want to risk waking Rachel from a much-needed sleep. She had looked positively haggard by the time we arrived home the afternoon before. I suspected that I had not looked much better.

Now that I felt fewer qualms over venturing into the village, I was eager to see if I could stock my pantry with something more substantial. Armed with Grant's discarded ration coupons, I started down the stairs. But I froze on the bottom step. Poking through the front door's mail slot were two letters.

My hands were shaking as I pulled the letters free. One was from my former boss at the shipping company. The other caused my heart to quaver. Instantly I recognized the handwriting. It was from my father.

I had not expected him to write me. I recalled how angry he had become during our quarrels about Grant. I knew he would have been mortified by how I had left without saying what I was doing or where I was going. By now my hands were trembling so I could hardly hold the envelope, much less open it. I was terrified that he would tell me not to come home. The thought left me scarcely able to breathe.

I set the letter from my boss down on the side table. That one could wait. Holding the letter from my father, I clenched my eyes shut, and prayed as hard as I had ever prayed in my entire life. I did not deserve anything better than to be disowned, I knew that. But I could also not help but pray for something more.

My stomach felt as frozen solid as the trees behind the orphanage. I slit the envelope and pulled out the single page. Daddy had never been one for a lot of words. Even so, the thinness of this letter drew the steel band around my chest even tighter.

I could put it off no longer. I unfolded the page and began to read. The words jarred so hard I dropped the sheet, and just stood there, trying to remember how to breathe.

I picked up the letter, and reread the page. A third time. Then more slowly. Through the closed door, I could hear the village church bells begin to peal. I lingered over the short note, the words vibrating in time to the ringing bell.

My dearest Emily,

I have asked your mother to allow me to write you first. Your letter arrived last night, and I have scarcely been able to sleep a wink. You have inherited my own stubborn strength, but you have grown far beyond anything I could ever hope to be. Your letter contained both newfound humility and a remarkable wisdom.

I am sorry this man hurt you so badly, but I am proud that you have managed to grow from the experience. Yes, proud. Your mother will write more tomorrow. This is all I wanted to say, except that I do so hope you will hurry home.

The leaves continue to fall from my calendar, each passing day marking the void your absence has caused in our lives.

With love, Dad.

I crushed the letter to my heart, wanting to shout, to cry, to sing out loud. Instead, I offered a single note of joyful thanks to the Lord above, then opened the door and stepped into the new day. I was instantly blinded by the sun.

AS ALWAYS, THERE were lines in front of every store. And, as usual, I could feel the eyes turn toward me as I strolled along the sidewalk. Today they did not bother me, not even when I joined the line at the grocer's and a trio of ladies turned to stare and whisper. I recognized them as having been among the group standing before the church on New Year's Eve. The Grim Brigade, Rachel had called them. As I observed them from the corner of my eye, with their tight mouths and hunched shoulders and angry looks, I decided they deserved the title. They certainly did look grim.

Turning away, I tried to focus my thoughts on the good things that had happened. My family loved me. The children had been inoculated. They would be getting better. A few might even be adopted. The sun was shining. Even so, I could feel the trio's whispered words cross the distance and strike me like darts.

I pulled the second letter from my pocket, the one from my boss at the shipping company, and used it as a shield. The letter held about what I had expected. The man was sympathetic, but also irritated—he had done so much to find me a way over to England. Naturally, he wrote, he would do all he could to find me a position. Or he could be called upon to write a recommendation. But as to a passage back, his connections were all for places going the other way. I sighed and stuffed the page back into my pocket.

"Oh, hello, Emily. Didn't see you standing there."

I looked up. The woman who had joined the queue behind me was Kate, the mistress of the night shift. Tears streaked her broad face. Instantly, concern over her pushed my own distress aside. I knew she had a boy who had not yet returned from Singapore. "What's the matter?"

"Oh, it's silly." She lifted the news magazine she was

holding. "There's this article on the DP crisis. I suppose you've heard about it."

"Who hasn't?" DPs, as displaced persons were known, had been streaming in from Eastern Europe ever since the fighting had stopped last May. According to what the papers said, there were millions and millions of them. Some were survivors of the death camps. Others were fleeing Stalin's army. Still others had seen their villages destroyed, their livestock killed, and had taken to the streets in search of food. Whole cities were on the move to nowhere.

"There were these pictures; here, have a look for yourself." Before I could object that I already had enough to worry about, Kate thrust the page under my nose.

Two photographs were set side by side. The first was of a train station, or what once had been one. The building itself had been bombed to rubble. The railroad tracks were lost beneath a sea of people. Thousands and thousands of them, huddled under makeshift tents, wrapped in rags, freezing on the snow-covered ground. I asked weakly, "Where is this?"

"Do you know, I didn't even get that far." She pointed at the second picture. "That one stopped me cold."

The photograph was of a dozen or so children, all of them trying to share two blankets. They were lying side by side, tight as sardines in a can. Snow had fallen while they lay, dotting the tattered cover with white. All but two of the children were still asleep, their faces almost lost beneath heaps of rags used to keep their ears and noses warm. But two girls looked up at the camera. They were perhaps eight or nine years old. One of them was flaxen-haired, the other dark. Hunger and fatigue and fear had turned them into twins. Especially their eyes.

"They look so much like our own little ones," the woman sniffled.

"Hmph." One of the trio sniffled loudly. "My Jim warned you at that first council meeting, you were getting in over your head, taking on that orphanage."

"There's too many of them," another agreed. "Your lot can't save the world on your own."

Kate reddened. "We certainly won't be having any help from you, now, will we?"

"I do my best to avoid lost causes and futile gestures," the first replied loftily.

"Aye, and it's a grand thing to see them finally clearing those wastrels out," her friend agreed. "Good riddance to bad rubbish, I say."

I did not join in the ensuing argument. The pair of images lingered, making a mockery of this petty gibing. The impressions stayed with me as I stood in line at the butcher's, and then the bakery. The eyes and the whispers were still there, but I did not have room for them. I felt as though the girls were trying to communicate with me, or perhaps it was God speaking through them. And I felt ashamed that, try as I might, I could not understand what was being said.

EIGHTEEN

I'm afraid the woman was correct, at least about one thing," Colin chided gently over dinner that night. "You can't go about trying to save the world."

"Oh, I know that." Yet the feeling of missing some vital message had stayed with me throughout the day. That and the image of those two girls. I wanted Colin to understand. For some reason, it was vital to try and share the power that photograph held for me. "It wasn't two strangers I saw there on the page. It was two of our girls."

Colin nodded slowly. "I see what you mean. And it very well could have been, you know. For some reason, the train stations have become gathering points for DPs."

"Not the station. It wasn't the setting at all." Trying to explain it to him was helping me draw it into focus for myself. As was the intent way he listened. "It was the *look*. Their expression and their gaze and the way I was staring at two totally different faces, but really seeing just one set of experiences . . . Oh, I don't know. I can't seem to explain myself at all."

Colin suggested, "Perhaps you feel like you were seeing into the past of those children who have been given into our care."

"That's it," I said, and was filled with the pleasure of being with someone who understood, who cared enough to *want* to understand me. "That's it exactly."

We were seated in the White Hart Inn, a riverside establishment dating back to the sixteenth century. Like most village inns, there were two main rooms—the public bar with its raw wood floors and louder voices, and the more subdued atmosphere of the carpeted parlor. Colin and I were seated near the fireplace, warmed by the flames and the company. We had just completed a wondrous concoction called venison stew; while there had been little meat to be found, the publican's wife had managed to elevate the common carrot and stalk of celery to wondrous levels. I was as pleasantly full as I had been since my arrival in England.

An image coalesced from the recesses of my thoughts. "I just thought of something. Did you notice how few of the children cried over the injections?"

"They were doing a jolly good job of wailing there at the start," Colin pointed out.

"While they were afraid, yes," I countered. "But once we had them calmed down, most didn't make a sound when they were inoculated."

"What are you saying, Emily?"

"It struck me as odd at the time, but you know how busy we all were. And then I thought of it again this afternoon. I found myself thinking of the way Annique watched me as the doctor gave her the injection."

"She just sat there in my arms," Colin recalled. "Didn't move a muscle."

"When I saw that photograph in the magazine, what I really saw was Annique. Her and all the others," I went on. "It brought home to me just how much they've gone through, these children."

"Bringing them to the point," Colin added for me, his face somber, "where they do not even cry over a needle and an injection and a strange doctor."

"Not unless they're scared," I finished quietly.

We sat there, silent for a long moment. Then Colin straightened with a sigh and rubbed his neck. I asked, "Are you all right?"

"I've been feeling a little tired lately."

"No wonder," I told him. "You really ought to slow down."

He smiled and changed the subject with, "You know, the hardest time for me was when we could not give the children a Christmas."

"What?" I cried. "Nothing at all?"

"There wasn't much of a Christmas for any of us," Colin said. "Most of our soldiers are still overseas, waiting for places on too few boats home. Rationing was worse than ever. Presents were lean on the ground, let me tell you. The whole town seemed dressed for Christmas in Land Army colors—brown, beige, gray, and lots of black." His face seemed to age as he spoke. "It seemed like the sweetness had gone from life. I had my Christmas with a friend who runs the parish church in Bottley, and a grim affair it was indeed. The only way his wife managed a Christmas dinner at all was because we butchered Adolf."

I stared at him. "Did what?"

"Adolf, the house pig," Colin explained. "Long overdue for the pot, if you ask me. Tough as a wild boar raised on shoe leather." He tried for a smile. "Christmas was a perfectly miserable time, if you want to know the truth. I spent the entire day running from one tragic household to the next. It was the first Christmas since the war ended, and so many families would never be whole again."

"But the children," I protested.

"There was simply so little of everything left," Colin said apologetically. "Besides which, we could not communicate with them. So we simply treated the day as any other, searching for enough food to keep their little bodies alive, and hoping for things to improve."

I sipped from my cup, wondering why it seemed as though his words were connected to the magazine picture and my own unheard message. Finally I pushed the confusion aside, and asked, "When can we expect to see your photographs?"

"Three days, perhaps four." His face drew longer lines. "That is, unless they need me on one of their empty treks to London."

Abruptly a shadow was cast over our evening. We had tried hard not to speak of our worries, but I knew the topic was bound to rise to the surface sooner or later. It was always there, hovering just beyond the reach of the fire and our cozy table. "There's been no change, then?"

"None at all, I'm afraid." Colin sighed and leaned back. "Even the mayor and his entourage have found nothing but a series of closed doors to their entreaties."

Before I could speak, the bartender came hurrying over. "Sorry to disturb you, but the operator's putting a call through."

Colin started to rise. "Won't be a moment."

"Not you, Vicar. It's for the young lady here."

I jerked upright. "Me?"

"If you're Miss Emily sitting with the vicar, it is indeed."

Confused, I followed him back. The phone was a wooden box hung from the central pillar, with a black Bakelite earpiece hanging from a long cord. I fitted the receiver to my ear, and raised up on tiptoes so I could say into the mouthpiece, "Hello?"

"This is Mabel at the booking agency. Oh, my dear, you wouldn't believe the trouble I've had tracking you down. First I tried the orphanage, and they told me to call Rachel, and she said you were with the vicar, but when I called the vicarage they said he had come here, and, well . . . Hello? Are you there?"

"Still here," I shouted back, feeling my cheeks flushing at the eyes watching me from both rooms.

"I can hardly believe it myself. Couldn't wait until tomorrow, of course, not with only six days left."

"Six days until what?"

"The ship sails, of course. Oh, goodness, I forgot to tell you that bit, didn't I? Yes, they've found you passage. On the *Brittany*. Sails from Portsmouth next Tuesday. Isn't that good news?"

I swallowed and managed to say, "Great."

"I knew you'd be pleased, that's why I didn't wait. You'll

need to stop in the office tomorrow, of course, there are forms to fill out and a deposit to pay."

"Of course. Thank you." I set the receiver back in slow motion. I did not want to turn around.

AS WE LEFT the inn, Colin steered me across the village's main crossroads and down toward the bridge. The night was so cold the wet air tasted metallic. An icy mist drifted in the utterly still air. Streetlights were golden globes floating above the cobblestone way. All was painted with their soft light. It was a special glow, granted only to this village, and only to this night. I shivered with the delicious pleasure of our lonely walk. "Why do you push yourself so hard, Colin?"

"Because it is in prayerful service that I find the closest connection to our Lord's command to love," he replied.

A lonely truck trundled by, and then the night and the silence closed back around us. We started across the bridge, its ancient stone turned luminous by the tall iron lamps. A bridge into the unknown, crossing over mist-clad waters. Colin said, "You've been so quiet since the call came for you. Is everything all right?"

I wish I knew, should have been my answer. But I could not speak. We stopped and leaned over the center of the bridge, staring at the dark waters flowing beneath us. So many questions, so many worries, so few answers.

"Emily?"

I did not turn toward him. What could I say, that I

might be leaving for America? That I might go away and abandon him and the children in their hour of need?

"I do wish you would say something."

But a sigh was all I could manage. America. It was strange how the possibility of going home was suddenly a problem and not a solution. I stared down at the waters and silently spoke a prayer, asking God for guidance. But the river remained a mystery, and I found no answers that night.

NINETEEN

The next day was busy before I even opened the door.

The doorbell startled me so that I spilled my tea all over my hand. I rushed down the narrow stairs. As I crossed the front room, a loud hammering began. I opened the door to find Rachel standing there, brandishing her cane. "Oh, there you are. Where on earth is your coat?"

"Upstairs. What's the matter?"

"Tell you on the way," she said, wheeling smartly about and stumping down the lane. "Hurry!"

I flew back upstairs, grabbed my coat and scarf, and raced to catch up. For a seventy-year-old woman leaning heavily on a cane, Rachel set a remarkable pace. "The orphanage called. Colin did not show up with his supplies this morning."

"So?"

"I fear the worst. He has never been late. Not once, not since this whole affair began."

Her harsh tone frightened me as much as her words. "Maybe he just overslept."

"Hardly likely. Regular as clockwork is our Colin."

Thankfully, the church courtyard's walk was graveled, for the world was frozen once again. The vicarage was a modest stone home built to match the church. The assistant pastor lived in what had once been the stables, the brick-and-beam walls so old they leaned heavily against the adjoining church. Dried stalks of wisteria climbed in haphazard profusion around the two lead-paned windows. Rachel knocked, then called loudly when Colin did not appear. "His truck is still here, so he—"

I shushed her, thinking I had heard something. There it was again, a faint cry from within. Something about the tone filled me with a fire of urgency. I pushed against the lever, then cried out, "It's locked!"

There was a low shuffling from within, then a crash, and finally the scrape of a key in the lock. I pushed open the door, and gasped at the sight of Colin standing in his nightshirt, leaning heavily upon the door. "What on earth is the matter?"

"Pushed myself too hard, I'm afraid." His complexion was gray and waxy. "Spoke with Bradley, the American pilot, yesterday evening. Something has come up, and he needed the photographs delivered to him this morning."

"So you stayed up all night to develop them." Rachel was as cross as I had ever seen her. She raised her cane once more to brandish it in his face. "Colin Albright, of all the silly messes, did you even for one moment think . . ."

Colin gripped the front of his nightshirt, and started to sink. I flung my arms about him for support. "Help me get him to the bed!"

Rachel and I managed to half-walk, half-drag him back into the bedroom. As I straightened the bedcovers, Rachel went next door to the vicarage in order to phone the doctor. Colin's complexion and his shortness of breath and the way he kept holding his chest worried me terribly. "Is there anything I can get you?"

"Photographs," he gasped. "Airfield."

I stared down at him. "What on earth is so important about those pictures?" Bradley's family had mentioned finding people willing to adopt a few of our children. "Why *all* the photographs?"

But Colin could only respond with a shake of his head. His gaze held such a desperate appeal, I could not bring myself to object any more. "All right. Where are they?"

"Darkroom." He pointed to a door in the side wall. I walked over and discovered a windowless cubbyhole that had been turned into a makeshift laboratory. Trays of rank-smelling chemicals lay across the table, and overhead was strung a series of wires with coat hangers. A few pictures still hung there, all of them showing me with one of the children. There was something about my expression that made the moment and Colin's illness even more poignant.

He called hoarsely from the bed, "Box. Take it to Fred."

The carton of photographs was there at my feet. Gingerly I released those still hanging and added them to the pile. It felt very uncomfortable to see so many images of myself.

As I carried it back into the other room, he groaned, "Fred."

"I heard you the first time."

The front door opened and Rachel entered. "The doctor's on his way."

I walked up to her and said, "Stay with him while I go call Fred. Colin's all in a lather that these get off." I glanced back to the bedroom. "Working all night, collapsing, then ordering me around over a bunch of pictures. He's just impossible."

"Of course he is, my dear," Rachel said, patting my arm. "He's a man, now, isn't he?"

THE DAY PASSED in a blur. And the day after that. And the third day. I never realized just how much Colin did until I tried to do it myself.

I was surrounded by things left undone. Whatever I did was not enough. For every task I finished, another dozen were added to my list.

Finally, on the evening of the third day, I managed to stop by the travel agency. I found poor Mabel beside herself. She leaped from her seat and demanded, "Where have you been?"

"Everywhere. Something has—"

"But I was expecting you the day before yesterday! I need you to fill out the forms, I need your deposit!"

"I'm not going."

She did her best imitation of a goldfish out of water. "You what?"

As swiftly as I could I explained what had happened to Colin. "I need to stay and help out."

She fell into her chair like a dropped sack. "My dear, do you have any idea—"

I waved it away. I did not want to hear. I did not want to be tempted away from the decision I had already made. The night before I had written my family a long letter, so tired I could scarcely keep my eyes open, but doing my best to explain what was happening. "Can you transfer my booking to another ship?"

Once more the mouth opened and closed without a sound. Eventually she squeaked, "I beg your pardon?"

"No, I guess that would be asking too much." A thought occurred to me. "Could I use your phone?"

Only when the operator came on the line did Mabel finally find her voice once more. "You are actually going to refuse this?"

"Maybe not." I spoke into the receiver, "Can you connect me to the American airfield, please?"

The wait for Bradley Atwater to come on the line seemed to go on forever. I avoided Mabel's gaze, and tried to ignore her rising volume of protests. When the midwestern twang drawled out a hello, I felt a vast flood of relief.

"Brad, it's Emily Robbins here."

"Emily!" He seemed to tense up at the sound of my voice. I decided that was no real surprise, since he only heard from me when something was wrong. "Is everything all right?"

"No, not really."

"How's the reverend doing?"

"The doctor says he's out of danger. He just needs to rest. But that's not—"

"Any word on the kids?"

His question seemed to hammer at me. Or perhaps it was the strain of the decision confronting me. Or perhaps simply because I was tired from carrying this crazy load. Whatever the reason, I felt a sudden burning to my eyes. "They're supposed to start moving them the week after next."

"Say, that's not good." He turned and relayed the information to someone standing nearby. There was a rising murmur of voices, before Brad came back and said, "We can't let that happen, Emily."

"I don't know what else we can do," I said, blinking back tears. Nine days from now, the first trucks were scheduled to arrive. The Ministry would move the children and close the orphanage in three weeks. The official notice hung from the bulletin board in our kitchen. "The mayor and the town council have worn out their welcome all over London. And it hasn't done a bit of good."

And when the children left, I wanted to add, there would be nothing left to hold me here. Nothing to fill the empty days. I could not look up at Mabel. Not without seeing a reflection of the other voice ringing through my head, the one that kept saying that I was a fool to pass up this chance. A purebred, hundred-proof fool.

I pushed away the thoughts and worries and hesitations with all the force I could muster. "That's not why I'm calling. I have a berth on a liner leaving in three days."

The news seemed to catch Brad flatfooted. "A berth?"

"A cabin. But with Colin doing so poorly, and the orphanage . . ." I had to stop and force another breath around the fist clenching my chest. "I was wondering if your church was still interested in taking a couple of our orphans."

"My church." Brad's voice slowed to a crawl. "A couple."

"You told me they might be willing to adopt them." I felt like I was pushing against an unseen wall. "This is a way to get them to America, don't you see?"

"Emily . . ." He seemed utterly at a loss for words. "I haven't . . . I mean, it's not yet . . ."

"I understand," I said, and I did. In a flash of insight, I felt as though the message was being scrolled across my heart. "Sorry to bother you."

"Emily, wait—"

I hung up the phone, and lifted my gaze to Mabel. I understood now. This was *my* decision. There was no way around it, nor anything to take its place. I took the hardest breath of my entire life, and said quietly, "I'm sorry, I can't go. Not now. Too many people are counting on me."

"But, my dear—"

"Mabel, I have to see this through to the end. I have to." My resolve was too weak to listen to her protests. I rose to my feet and started for the door. "Ask them if they will transfer the place to a later boat. It can't hurt. And if they can't," I opened the door, hesitated a moment, and finished weakly, "then they can't. And thank you."

I took a few steps down the sidewalk, scarcely believing

what I had just done. Yet as I walked, the sadness and regret I expected to hit me never arrived. Instead, I felt light, as though an unseen burden had been taken from me. Something so much a part of me that I had not even noticed its presence, until it was no longer there.

TWENTY

Everyone said it was my idea. But that was not true, well, not really. I didn't wish to be held responsible for something I had never really even meant to say.

The next day, we were at the entrance by the orphanage kitchen, unloading a horsecart full of eggs and milk. Rachel was standing alongside the front wheel, holding the horse's reins and chattering with the farmwife. "I have never seen anything quite like it," Rachel was saying.

"The village has done been cut in two," the farmwife agreed, handing me down another crate with straw-packed eggs. "Them that's glad to see the back of these little ones were ahead for a time. Dancing about they were, acting like they'd seen it coming."

"Not anymore," Rachel said, patting the pony's flank. "Watching those people who haven't lifted a finger gloat so, well, it certainly lit a fire under the others."

"Not half," the woman agreed. She was a spindly thing, all wiry muscle and easy strength. Her hands had broadened and flattened with years of hard work, and her face beneath the winter bonnet was chapped and toughened. But her smile was brilliant, and her eyes clearest blue. "Heard more'n a little grumbling these past weeks. All dried up now, it has. Folks didn't know how much these kittens meant to the town, not until it's come time to see them off."

"People I've not spoken to before have been coming up to me," Rachel went on, "asking if there isn't something they could do to save the children from the DP camps."

"Shame they didn't ask that a while back," the woman said, handing down the last of the milk tins. She straightened and looked around the empty cart. "Hard to believe this'll almost be my last delivery."

"Oh, don't say that," Rachel cried. "You'll have me all weepy again, and that won't do the children a bit of good."

"They know something's up," I agreed. "I can see some of the old shadows coming back."

"Not much we can do about that," the farmwife said in her practical no-nonsense manner. "Still, I'll be sorry to see the tykes go. Strange how giving to this lot has left me feeling so rich."

"Oh, that reminds me." I raced past the women stacking produce in our larder, and pulled the cash box off the top shelf. I came back outside. "My memory has been like a sieve lately."

"As hard as you've been running," Rachel responded, "it's a miracle you can remember your own name."

The farmwife's eyes widened as she watched me extract a wad of bills. "What you got there, now?"

"The Ministry finally came through with some funds," I said, and could not keep the bitterness from my voice. "I got a call from the bank yesterday afternoon."

"She was up half the night, trying to bring our books up to date," Rachel added, shaking her head. "If she doesn't watch out, we'll have her laid out there alongside Colin."

I counted out the money, and handed it over. "We can't thank you enough for all you've done."

The farmwife looked wondrously at the bills in her hand, and then back at me. "You're paying me?"

"I had to make a guess," I told the farmwife. "You stopped leaving chits a few weeks ago. But I think that's pretty close."

"Wait till my Bert hears about this." She stuffed the notes in a pocket, and slowly shook her head. "Never thought I'd see the day come when I'd be sad to get paid."

"You're not alone," Rachel said. "I took the money by the grocer's this morning. His wife actually broke down and wept. Said it hadn't seemed that the children were actually leaving until right then."

"Everybody's talking about how they'd like to do something," the woman said. "Just wish we knew what."

For some reason, I found myself thinking back to the day I had stood in line at the grocer's, looking at the magazine and staring into those children's eyes. And how I had been unable to understand the message that was whispered to my heart. I closed the cash box and turned around, saying as I passed through the doorway, "We could always give them a Christmas."

I set the cash box back in place, then returned outside, only to find the two women standing there, staring open-mouthed at me. Finally Rachel said, "What did you just say?"

"I suppose it is silly," I said, ashamed now that I had spoken at all. "It's just, well, the other day Colin was telling me how sad everyone had been at Christmas. And how nothing was done for the children."

"A village Christmas," the farmwife murmured.

"But it's the middle of February," Rachel protested.

"Aye, so it is." The farmwife reached down and took the reins from Rachel's hands. "And what difference does that make, I ask you?"

She settled into the wagon's seat, clicked to the horses, and said, "I'll be having a word with my Bert over this."

"A CHRISTMAS FOR the children." Colin beamed at me. "Emily, it's a positively splendid idea."

"It wasn't an idea, not really. Just something that sort of popped out."

"Well, it's just as well you don't wish to lay claim." Colin watched as I moved about his little kitchen. "It's the village's idea now. I've had a half-dozen people stop by to describe what they want to do, or have done, or organize, or help put together. Almost as though everyone has been waiting for just this way to put their feelings into action."

I didn't know what to say. Colin was seated at his kitchen table, watching as I heated up a supper brought back from the orphanage. I had taken to having my dinner there, checking on him before night settled in, and going over what I would need to do on the morrow. I found myself looking forward to these times alone together. Occasionally during those busy days I would find I had stopped whatever I was doing, just thinking about him and something he had said, or the way he smiled, and the thought would warm me.

He was up and walking about now, and his color had steadily improved. But he remained too weak for the doctor to allow him back to his duties at the orphanage, something that chafed mightily. But in these quiet secret moments, I was glad in a way that he still needed my care. Even though taking over his chores tired me so, and despite my worries over his heart, I was glad for how this had brought us together in such a special way.

I pointed out, "The children won't understand what's going on. Or that it's supposed to be a Christmas party."

"Oh, they might, you know. We can easily afford to hire an interpreter for the day, now that the Ministry has finally come through." His smile turned mischievous. "I can see no reason not to spend a bit of the leftover funds on a little feast. Besides which, the older ones are making progress with their English. They'll understand enough to know that all is well."

I set the plate down in front of him, but he continued to stare up at me. "That is the essential message of Christmas, wouldn't you agree?" Colin's smile warmed me to my very core. "For those who accept God's gift, all is well."

TWENTY-ONE

When Marissa came downstairs the next morning, Christmas was there to greet her.

"Ooooh." She walked into the living room, where brightly wrapped presents were spread out around a tree with its cheerfully blinking lights. Silver streamers caught the fire's glow and transformed the tree into a green-and-gold beacon.

Her grandmother came up behind her, set down the two steaming mugs of cocoa, and gave her a warm hug. "Merry Christmas, darling."

"Merry Christmas, Gran." Marissa could not help glancing at the mantel clock over her grandmother's shoulder. "I'm afraid you're going to have to wait a little while for your present though."

The hug tightened. "Child, I am holding the best present I could possibly ask for."

She stood there, wrapped in her grandmother's arms, feeling that they were both different people from those who had come together just a few short days ago. It was not just Marissa who had been changed, at least not in her own eyes. Her grandmother had become more than just an older relative. She was now a woman with experiences and wisdom all her own.

Sharing these gifts of a life that was Gran's and Gran's alone had eased away some of the harsh lines that had creased her face since Granpa's funeral. Somehow, the act of sharing was changing Gran as well. The thought warmed Marissa right down to her toes.

It was only the phone's ringing that opened Gran's arms. "That will be your mother."

Marissa accepted the phone and spoke with each of her family in turn, wishing them all a Merry Christmas, trying to put as much heart as she could in the words. Pretending to be excited over what her brothers received came easy; all she had to do was direct her impatient ferment in their direction. When she set down the phone, she glanced at the clock once again, and released a sigh. It was going to be a long three hours.

Gran misunderstood her sigh. "You mustn't be sad, child. The distance between us and them really isn't that great. Here in our hearts, they are with us still."

"I know," she said, not correcting her grandmother. In any case, Gran was partly right. "But could we wait a little while before we open our presents?"

"If you like." A small smile played over Gran's features. "What should we do in the meantime?"

Marissa grinned. "You know exactly what I want to do."

"Well, I suppose I should make you some breakfast while we talk." Gran rose to her feet. "Are you tired of oatmeal yet?"

That final week before the children were scheduled to be farmed out to camps passed in a continuous blur. I worked until I could work no longer, then fell into my bed, sometimes not even bothering to undress. The village was a hive of activity.

There were delegations of every make and model, from farmers to housewives to the entire village council, all traveling to London to beseech the Ministry to let the orphanage stay open. The thought of our children being dispatched to an array of nameless DP camps left everyone distraught. But nothing did any good. I could tell whenever someone had just returned from London, for they walked with shoulders slumped and face turned down. It was a very hard time for us all.

Perhaps because of that, people poured an enormous amount of energy into preparing for the Christmas fete, scheduled for the day before the first buses would arrive to transport children to the camps.

Colin remained too weak to return to the orphanage. But there was nothing we could do to keep him from helping around the village. Nor did we try. It was an important activity for all of us. We took strength from seeing the preparations take shape, and from being able to talk about the fete. It took the edge off what otherwise would have been an unbearable tragedy.

Then came the day. There have been a number of special moments in this life of mine. But this was *the day*. From the very outset, it was a time set apart, an instant lifted up by God's heavenly angels. That is the way I saw it, even at first light, when I rose from my bed and stepped out onto my little balcony to watch the river flow silent and strong. As I stood there, drinking in the early morning light, I heard the most remarkable sound, a whooshing prism of musical tones. It sounded as though angels were humming in unison. I turned in time to see six white swans come sailing by, their outstretched wings catching the still air and making it sing in their passage.

I had taken to reading the Gospels with my first cup of tea, a time of quiet shared with my Lord. Usually it was the only peaceful moment of my entire day. That morning, I read about the poor woman who shamefully tossed her two tiny coins into the temple's coffers, and how the Lord had blessed her for giving out of her poverty.

I sat and sipped my steaming cup, and thought of this quiet little village and how they had struggled to make room for the children. How they had never asked for recognition or thanks, how they had scarcely had enough for themselves. How their own hearts were seared and scarred by wounds and loss. Yet even so, they had given what love they had, and in so doing had offered me the grace of both healing and newfound wisdom.

I read no more that day.

I PUT ON my coat and scarf, and went downstairs, where I discovered a letter peeking through the mail slot. There were quite a few letters these days—from my family mostly, but also from friends back home who had heard of my sadness and offered the only comfort they could. So I was already out on the lane and halfway to Rachel's door before I glanced down at the envelope, and recognized the handwriting. A bolt of lightning could not have struck me harder.

Grant Rockwell.

With numb fingers I tore open the envelope, and read the impossible. Grant wrote that he wanted to see me. He was not sure how he felt about anything, but he missed me and he wanted to see me. If I agreed, he would make a trip to Arden in a week or so.

He wanted to see me.

I sat through a second cup of tea with Rachel, and forced my jumbled mind to discuss all we needed to do that day. But it was as if I was hearing her through the noise of a machine shop. My mind kept shouting out the incredible, impossible news.

And yet my heart was silent. I left Rachel's and started down the lane. These days, she traveled to the orphanage alone. I usually made a quick visit to Colin, then did the shopping before traveling up with the morning bus.

As I walked through the quiet village churchyard, I felt a silent waiting deep within my heart. My mind kept up its frantic tugging, shouting with excitement over the amazing letter burning a hole in my coat pocket. Yet the desire to see Grant was overlaid by all that had happened to me.

In the middle of the courtyard, I stopped. The morning sky was slightly overcast, the clouds as thin as gauze. The sun was gentled to a grand golden orb, and already the day was warmer than it had been in weeks. The grass growing up around the ancient tombstones was brown, the air sweet with the odor of awakening earth. I stood there for a long time, listening to the tangled voices within me.

Finally I closed my eyes and prayed. There was no way I could solve this dilemma myself, I said, and begged the Lord to help me. As I prayed, I sensed a quieting of all my inner noise. I kept my eyes closed even after the prayer had ended, feeling the silence grow and expand, until there was simply no longer room for the clamor.

I opened my eyes. There before me stood a tombstone. The letters had been washed away by the years and the weather. For a brief instant, I imagined that there upon the pale smooth stone were written new words. Words declaring the death of a relationship, one that had never been granted the chance to grow to fruition. It could not be unearthed. It was gone.

I felt no need for tears. My chest did not burn with the tragic remorse of earlier days. There was a sorrow, yes, but it was the quiet sadness of visiting a well-tended grave.

After a time, I turned and continued on to the vicarage. As had become my habit, I knocked and then let myself in. A voice from the kitchen called out, "Is that you?"

"Good morning, Colin." I moved straight for the fireplace. "How are you today?"

"Better. Just a minute, I'm up to my elbows in washing-up suds." When I did not appear in the doorway, he called out, "What are you doing?"

"It's chilly in here. And damp. I want to start a fire."

"Well, come, let me see you."

"I won't be a minute." I did not want to go in there. Not yet. Hastily I bundled up several pages of newspaper, then set the kindling and a pair of logs on top. I lit it with a kitchen match. When it was burning well, I fumbled in my pocket and brought out Grant's letter. I stared at it for a moment, then reached out and dropped it into the flames.

There was the sharpest pang, as though a ribbon of steel had been drawn from my chest. Then nothing. No further pangs, no sadness, nothing except a sense of overwhelming rightness.

I rose, and turned and found Colin standing there in the doorway. He was dressed in a pair of old trousers, a shirt, a quilted robe, and tattered houseslippers. He gave me his sweet smile, and said, "But I didn't care to wait another moment. Good morning, Emily."

I stood and stared at him. This dear man, with his unruly hair and his bad heart and his quiet unassuming ways. A man who lived to give, and to do so with all the love he had. A rush of something new flooded me, an affection born of sweetness and sharing. And instantly I knew that here was something solid, something that could indeed remain and grow for a lifetime.

Colin cocked his head. "You have the strangest look on your face."

"I'm glad to see you're doing so much better," I said, my voice weak in my own ears.

"Indeed I am. Shall I make us a cup of tea?"

THE VILLAGE BUS let me off at the orphanage's tall stone entrance gates. I walked down the winding lane, sheltered beneath elms so ancient their girth could not have been encircled by three men. The branches creaked and weaved in the growing wind. I listened to my feet clip over the rounded stones, and breathed in the warm fragrant air. Beyond the empty branches, clouds cantered across the sky. My mind was filled with the wonder of having left behind invisible chains. And of what the future might hold in store for me.

As usual, upon my arrival I checked on the kitchen, received a list of tasks from Rachel, then went upstairs to visit Annique. She was doing much better, the brilliant sparkle gradually returning to her dark eyes. I walked down the sick-hall's central aisle, glorying in how many of the beds had been stripped of their linen, and their mattresses rolled up tight. Each empty bed was a joy beyond measure. Not even the fact that we had only two more days with these wonderful children could dim the feeling of triumph.

Annique was sitting up and waving frantically as I approached. I smiled my greeting, and sat down on the edge of her bed. "What is it?" She handed me the hairbrush.

I laughed. "I think you're well enough to do it yourself today." But she had already turned her back to me, so I began brushing the soft dark locks.

It was such a restful, intimate moment. The dark-haired pixie sat utterly still, and began humming a tune. It was a plaintive melody, the lilting rhythm unlike anything I had heard before. Softly she began to sing words I did not understand. I found myself wondering about all the secrets this child carried, all the memories that were a universe away from the here and now. What mother had taught this child these words? What had happened to her family, her home, her world?

When the hair was shining with the luster of youth, I set down the hairbrush and on an impulse untied the little ribbon from my own hair. I gathered up a plait by her right ear, and tied a bow. She turned around, touching the ribbon, cooing, holding her hands in front of her face in a parody of wishing she could look in a mirror. I rose to my feet. "I have a compact in my purse," I said. "I'll be right back."

Rachel found me in the little alcove we used as a volunteer's room, pawing through my purse. "There's someone downstairs for you."

"Do you have a compact? I must have left mine at home."

"I imagine so, dear." She reached into her purse and handed it over. "But I really think you should—"

"I'll be right down." I hurried out.

But when I arrived back at the sick-hall, I halted just inside the doors. Standing beside Annique's bed was Henryk, a boy who was sprouting into a strapping young lad. I could hear their laughter and excited chatter from where I stood. Quietly I let myself back out, and took my smile down the stairs.

TO MY SURPRISE, I found the two American airmen standing there in our front hallway. "Bob! Bradley! What on earth are you doing here?"

The two young men boasted grins that threatened to split their faces in two. "Searching for you," Bob announced cheerfully.

"Morning, Emily," Brad said. "How's the reverend?"

"Better. What has you two looking like the cat that swallowed the canary?"

For some reason my question only made them grin the harder. Brad turned to Bob and said, "You go first."

"If you say so," Bob said, his smile like the sun. "But it'd make more sense for you to have the honors."

"Naw, you lead on," Brad replied. "Otherwise your news might get lost in the shuffle."

"But she won't make heads or tails of it."

"Don't matter none." Their grins seemed to compete for size. "Got to tell her in little doses, don'tcha see. Too much and she'll choke like a horse trying to swallow an apple whole."

"Tell me what," I cried, feeling an infectious excitement.

"Somebody better get a move on," Brad drawled. "'Fore the lady jumps out of her skin."

"Okay, okay," Bob sighed in mock resignation. "So I'm telling. Emily, you know what a Constellation is?"

"You mean, like the Milky Way?"

"He means," Brad said, "like the plane."

"Biggest workhorse in the sky," Bob went on. "Sucker can lift a ten-ton load. Ten tons."

"Gotta see that baby in action to believe it," Brad said. "First time I sat in the cockpit, I woulda taken bets it'd never leave the ground."

"Somebody is about to get the sharp end of a stick," I snapped, "unless I hear what this is all about, and right quick!"

"I got one," Bob announced. And stopped. The pair just stood and grinned at me.

"One what?" I shouted in utter exasperation.

"The plane," Bob replied. "Been working like a loony, trying to set it up. Finally came through this morning." He seemed to take vast satisfaction in my confused look, and turned back to Brad to declare, "Told you she wouldn't understand."

"She will soon enough."

Rachel appeared in the doorway, and demanded, "Why on earth is everyone clamoring so?"

"Hey there, Rachel," Brad said.

"Nice weather we're having," Bob said around his grin.

"Never mind that," I cried. "What is going on?"

Brad gave a mock sigh, and unbuttoned his shirt pocket. He drew out a flimsy sheet of yellow paper, and handed it over. "This here is prop number one."

With trembling hands, I opened the page, and read the impossible.

CHURCH LED BY PRAYER AND FASTING TO FIND HOMES FOR YOUR CHILDREN STOP SEND AS MANY AS YOU CAN STOP LETTER FOLLOWS STOP
ELDER BRADLEY ATWATER SENIOR
INDIANA MISSION FELLOWSHIP

Rachel demanded, "What does it say?"

Numbly I handed over the page. Brad was already reaching into his other pocket and came out with a second envelope, this one white and several pages thick. "Prop number two. Arrived by one of our flights yesterday afternoon."

The letter was from Brad's father, informing us that he had taken up our cause with the church's statewide board. It seemed that a number of their churches wanted to do something to help heal the wounds caused by war. Hearing about our orphans, the Elder Bradley Atwater wrote, had united these church members under the banner of a shared cause.

I looked up. "Why haven't you said anything before now?"

"Had to make sure we could pull it off."

Rachel's seamed face appeared unable to find any reason to lift up in hope. "I'm afraid it's all going to be for naught," she said quietly. "The Ministry will refuse to grant us the necessary papers. I feel sure of it."

"Yeah, that's why we had to wait for this other stuff," Bob agreed, his grin not slipping a notch.

"What are you talking about?" I demanded.

Brad asked, "You ever heard of the *Stars and Stripes*?"

"The American military newspaper. Of course."

"Well, we talked to the colonel who runs our base. And he talked to the general. And the general got on the horn to the *Stars and Stripes*. And they got on to," Brad had to stop and share his joy with his mate. "Who was it they woke up next?"

"I think it was the radio guy."

"Yeah, that's right. NBC. And they talked to the, oh, heck, now I've forgotten."

"*Times*," Bob offered with vast satisfaction. "The *London Times.*"

"Yeah. And that lady, she got so hot over hearing about what the Ministry's been dragging you folks through, she called some buddy over at Movietone News." Brad patted his hair into place. "Bob and me, we're gonna be movie stars."

"They spent almost an hour filming an interview with us," Bob added. "Asked us near 'bout everything you can imagine and then some."

Rachel and I shared openmouthed stares before the older woman managed, "I don't know what to say."

"Whatever it is, you gotta make it quick," Bob replied. "That is, if you want to be there when the boom falls in London."

"The general and the colonel and the press are all scheduled to land on the Ministry beaches," Brad informed us proudly. "Just after lunch."

"And there's one thing they teach us early on in the army," Bob added, ushering us toward the front door. "You don't want to keep a general waiting."

TWENTY-TWO

There was no hope of keeping Colin from coming along. He simply stopped all possible arguments by climbing into the U.S. Army truck's rear compartment and shouting, "Tallyho!"

"Sounds good to me," Brad called back, slamming his door and jamming the truck into gear. "Whatever it was he just said."

Rachel sat up front with Brad, while Bob bounced and swung about with us in the back. When Colin caught sight of my cross look, he grinned and said, "I simply can't imagine not being there for this."

"Don't get your hopes up just yet," Rachel called from the front. "Nothing's guaranteed when it comes to dealing with the Ministry."

"Precisely," Colin agreed, reaching out with both his hands. "I can think of no finer moment for us all to join together in prayer."

WE MADE QUITE a sight, ppearing at the Ministry's entrance barrier with the dozen or so newspeople in tow. The officers had arrived as promised, flanked by soldiers standing at the sort of ramrod attention generated by people of impossible rank. I watched as Bob and Bradley popped from our truck and snapped off crisp salutes of their own. The three men who responded possessed more stars and brass than I had ever seen in person before.

The eldest of them, a gray-haired gentleman with knife-edged features and three stars on his lapels, looked at me and said, "Are you the lady responsible for this?"

"No sir," I replied, turning to where Rachel clambered down, leaning on Colin for support. "That is—"

"She most certainly is," Rachel countered, and used her cane to stump over. "Emily Robbins is the force behind involving you gentlemen in our plight, right from the very beginning."

"I see." Eyes like cannon barrels swiveled back to focus upon me. "Well, Miss Robbins, I'd pin a medal on you, if I could only figure out which one."

"Hold it right there, General." A man wearing a rumpled suit and holding a huge camera shouldered his way to the front. "Shake her hand, will you? That's it. Come on, lady, give us a big smile. No, no, your hair's fine, just leave it and smile. Okay, one more."

"Time enough for that later," the general motioned toward the crowd of newspeople gathering attention. "Let's get this show on the road."

It was clearly not every day that an American general, flanked by a military entourage and the international press, came to call upon Ministry officials. As we walked through the imposing front hall, we saw a senior official accompanied by a pair of dark-suited assistants come scurrying down the front stairs and spill out toward us. "General, excuse me for not being out front to greet you, but I only just received word that the American ambassador had personally called the Minister himself and—"

"No problem." He accepted the handshake, turning to allow more pictures to be taken. "These are mostly newsfolk, I don't know who all has joined us. But we've got to find some place for the Movietone people to set up their cameras."

"Their . . . Of course." He flicked a hand toward one of his assistants. "See these good people up to the main conference hall."

"Of course, Deputy Minister."

"Now then, General, if you will just come this way, I will be happy to show you—"

"You haven't met Miss Robbins, have you?"

"Why, no." The deputy minister squinted down at me. I gave up trying to put my hair back in order. Wind through the truck's canvas flaps had left it in total disarray. Not to mention the dusty state of my threadbare clothes. "I don't believe I've had the honor. How do you do."

"It's not me," I said weakly. "Reverend Albright and Rachel Ballard, they're responsible for the orphanage."

"The orphanage," the deputy minister said slowly. "I'm sorry, General, I was informed that this meeting was in reference to an issue of national importance."

"It is," the general rapped out. "If you consider what the press is going to be writing about you and your work."

The deputy minister's mouth opened and shut a couple of times before finally coming out with, "I see."

"No, you don't. What we need here is the bureaucrat who's been responsible for trying to close down these people's orphanage." That intense gaze turned back toward me. "What was her name again?"

"Tartish," Colin replied for me. "Miss Hillary Tartish."

"That's the one." The general turned back to the official. "Now if I were you, I'd go see if you can find this woman, and let her try to explain exactly what she's been up to."

I TRIED NOT to gloat. Truly I did. But it was hard. Especially when the cameras were rolling, and Hillary Tartish was standing up there, trying to explain why we would not be allowed to ship the three hundred and eleven orphans to families who were eagerly awaiting them. Then I watched as the deputy minister overrode her, just silenced her with a single look, and said that he personally would see to expediting the required paperwork. I could not keep hold of a serious expression, not entirely. My smile kept popping into view. Such as when the cameras showed the deputy minister and the general shaking hands, with Colin and Rachel flanking them, and Miss Tartish backed into the shadows at the far corner of the room.

We were a quiet and happy lot on the way home. The joy carried us into the orphanage, and spread as we told each of the workers in turn. The children were soon running about, scampering from one of us to the other, as though drinking in our smiles and laughter and excited chatter. We tried hard to make them understand, taking a few of the older ones to one side, and in words as simple as we could make them, we described what was about to happen.

It was Henryk, the young man I had last seen seated on the side of Annique's bed, who first comprehended. I saw it happen. He was no longer a boy, not even if in years he could scarcely have been more than fifteen. His face had the hardened features of one forged upon the fires of relentless war. The instant he understood what we were saying, he leaped to his feet. His chair clattered over behind him, but he paid it no mind. His eyes widened as he looked from one of us to the other, searching with searing intensity.

Finally he whispered just one word, "*America?*"

"Yes." I shivered from the same power that was sending tremors through his spare frame. "That's right. All of you."

With trembling fingers he pushed himself away from the table, and stumbled for the door. We sat there, hearing him speak with one child after another. It was like listening to the gathering of some miraculous storm. Finally the power broke forth, spilling in lightning peals up and down the stairs, through the entire length and breadth of the house. Hundreds of racing feet, with shrill voices singing out one single word, over and over and over.

America.

TWENTY-THREE

The Christmas celebration did not come as a surprise to the children. It could not have. The villagers had decided the festival would be a way to celebrate the children's farewell. But we endured delay after delay in our preparations—first there were problems with the children's papers, then the plane could not come as planned, then the assembly in Indiana requested a bit more time. We spent the time preparing a little pageant for ourselves. It helped to have some amusing distraction to balance against the loss of our little charges. We were excited about how things were working out, but still saddened over this coming change.

The American fliers and their crews became a part of our daily routines, driving up with messages and news and food. Not to mention all the reporters. After the first series of articles appeared, other publications became interested in how a village had supported these children and then received help from the American army air corps, and how we had found three hundred homes for them in America. We cheerfully accepted the extra strain of their company. The more publicity we received, the more pliant the Ministry became. Anything that greased the government's skids was good news.

Finally, finally the day arrived. The tension was so thick the air was hard to breathe. The children reacted by growing solemn. Some understood more than others, but none could fathom why there were arguments among the staff, and tense voices in the hallway as we struggled to give them all baths. The little forms were blue and shivering, since only so much water could be heated on the stoves. Everything became too rushed, scrubbing them dry and trying to sort through the new clothes and have them ready on time.

By then the children knew that they were going to America, or at least they had heard the words. What they understood was that they were going away. Some were excited, most were afraid. Having us become so nervous and flustered did not help things at all.

At last we were as ready as we could be. The children no longer hid when things went wrong—the worst of their fears and wounds were healing. But there were furtive glances and quiet whimpers from the littlest as we herded them into the downstairs chambers and did one last head count.

"Three hundred and nine," said a very breathless Colin. "And I can't find Rachel."

"Two children missing." My heart sank. Annique. She had been one of the last to fall ill, and now was one of the last to get well. I raced up the stairs, almost colliding with Annique as she came out the door. Shyly she smiled at me, without releasing Henryk's hand. I pointed them down the stairs, and asked, "Rachel?"

"In here, my dear." I entered the sickroom, and found the older woman standing by the door. Her arms were crossed over her chest, and she was smiling slightly as she stared out over the room. "We have reached a watershed," she declared quietly.

The long rows of rolled-up mattresses stood as a testimony to days and nights of worry, hard work, and finally of success. The emptiness was sad, and yet one of the most satisfying sights I had ever seen. "I will miss them," I confessed.

"Oh, I was not speaking of the children," Rachel replied. "I suppose it is true with the children as well, although I personally can only see everything that is still left to be done." She turned to smile at me. "I was speaking of us, my dear. I owe you my heartfelt thanks."

"Me? What did I do?"

"You were the catalyst." Rachel enfolded me in her arms. "In the midst of your darkness, you allowed God to work through you. And look at the wonders the Lord has wrought in my own heart!"

THE VILLAGE HAD done the children proud.

The sun shone from a pristine blue sky upon our motley parade. Slowly we wound down the long hill from the orphanage to the river. The village's three buses had been pulled from their regular routes, and they led the retinue. Following them were the dairy's four milk vans, the backs emptied to make room for children. After them came nine hay wagons from local farms, two grocers' delivery trucks, the plumber's van, the sixteen private cars that had enough petrol for the journey, and Fred's taxi with its enormous black gas bag.

We chugged down the village High Street, encircled the little plaza before the Town Hall, and stopped with backfires and clouds of black smoke.

There was an instant of total silence, broken by a single whimper by one of the smaller children. They packed every square inch of the long array of vehicles. Moon-shaped eyes stared in utter bafflement at the hundreds of villagers lining the sidewalks and the town square. Then the bandleader raised his baton, and the village band broke into a vigorous tune of welcome.

That broke the ice. As we started to help the littlest children out of the transport, the villagers spilled toward us in a happy, chattering stream.

The children reacted by trying to hide behind our skirts. But there were not enough of us, and too many of the townsfolk.

Soon the plaza and the lane leading across to the church were full of milling, scrambling bodies. Local children led a group of the orphans, most of whom could not understand a word of what was being said, racing through the churchyard. The old vicar, a fussy gentleman who was delighted to leave most of the town duties to Colin, grew red in the face trying to shoo them off the old gravesites.

The villagers had dug out old Christmas bunting from some long-forgotten fete, and strung it from everything that would hold still. Many of the doors up and down the

High Street were festooned with holly wreaths. The American servicemen had set up a table where they were doling out orange slices and chocolates to the children. An excited storm of kids raced around, with sticky chocolate goo smeared over their faces.

The road to the bridge had been closed and all traffic diverted, so that a veritable feast could be laid out on trestle tables down the High Street. Much of the required funds had come from what was left of the Ministry's account. The army had given us a great deal, and the rest had come from various families. Everyone had brought something. After the weeks of hardship and scrounging, all that food set proudly down the center of the tables was very difficult to take in.

Every table had its own goose, roasted to a crisp golden brown and garnished with all sorts of hard-to-find fruit. There were hams and boiled eggs and three kinds of potatoes and a half-dozen vegetables. For dessert, heaps of good Christmas pudding wafted ginger and spices into the sunny air.

Our children were reluctant to sit down. They had difficulty believing that this feast was meant for them. Warily they circled the tables, staring round-eyed at all that wonderful food.

Finally we took some of the smaller ones by the hands, and settled them in place, and prepared plates for them. By each setting was a little paper crown, something found at every family Christmas dinner in England. As the children tried them on, some of the crowns slipped right over their ears and settled on their shoulders. All the crowd laughed at that. The older children watched with caution, until finally they grasped that they could have as much of everything as they liked. They scrambled for places and plates, then ate and laughed and chattered and ate.

For a while the adults remained silent, caught up in the miracle of the moment. We smiled and watched and shared in a time so full of joy and completion that there was little room for words.

Then the moment flowed on, and suddenly we were all talking and laughing, reaching across the table, passing the bowls and platters up and down. The band played tune after tune. When I felt I would burst if I took another bite, I rose from the table, only to find myself facing a shyly smiling Annique. She motioned with her arms, and I understood that she wanted to dance with me.

Together we walked over in front of the bandstand, where a few of the children were circling about in a laughing little ring. We clasped our arms and stepped to the lively tune, and I felt my face rise in the biggest smile I had ever known. There was so much joy in Annique's dark eyes, so much youth and newfound hope. I felt healed by the thought that I had had something to do with this young girl's blossoming. I felt renewed.

When the band stopped, I was startled by the sound of all the villagers clapping and shouting. Annique's hands flew up to cover her mouth, as we both realized they were clapping at us. My face turned crimson, and I felt an urge to run and hide.

But before my legs could carry me a single step, it seemed as though all the village had come out to join us on the makeshift dance floor. Annique was swept away by a grinning Henryk. I found myself hugging total strangers and laughing at jokes that were all but swept away by the surrounding noise. I watched the grocer's wife dancing with great gusto, pausing every now and then to check the seams of the stockings I had given her. And over at the corner of the crowd I spotted one of the Grim Brigade, only now she was tapping her toe and smiling slightly, or at least she did until she caught herself, then she stiffened and drew herself up straighter.

I danced with Brad and Bob and people I did not recognize, passed from hand to hand around the floor, until I finally arrived before Colin. There was something in his eyes, a new soft light, which left my heart squeezed with a joy and an anticipation unlike anything I had ever known before.

He reached into his pocket and handed me a brightly wrapped package. "Merry Christmas, Emily."

I was reluctant to take it. "Colin, you shouldn't—"

"To make up for what you lost," he said, then stopped in midflow as a blush rose from his collar to turn his face crimson. "That is, I wanted to get you something."

His dark vicar's suit was shiny with wear, and the cuff of the arm holding out the gift was frayed. I found myself swallowing a lump in my throat before I could manage, "This is the sweetest thing anyone has ever given me."

"You don't even know what it is yet."

"That doesn't matter." I accepted the gift, unwrapped

the small bottle of perfume, and gave him a smile from the depths of a very full heart. "I will treasure this always, Colin. This and everything behind it. Thank you so much."

Then it was the most natural thing in the world to reach out and embrace him. I wrapped my arms around his neck, not caring who saw me or what they said. Not then. I felt Colin hesitate, then relax and return my embrace. His arms felt so strong. So good and so solid and so *right*.

Finally we released one another and shared a quiet intimate smile. Then we began the process of herding everyone into the church.

There were nowhere near enough seats for everyone, but the grand old structure had volumes of room in the alcoves and crannies. As I helped gather the orphanage's little choir at the front, I could not keep them from turning and staring at the Christmas tree and the sign that hung high overhead.

Colin and the local schoolmistress had designed a huge Christmas card, which the village school had then painted for the orphans. With silver angels blowing trumpets from the two top corners, towering letters shouted out the message, *To Us a Savior Is Born*. The words had been translated into Russian, Polish, German, Czech, Romanian, and Hungarian. We had to stop and let the children laugh and point and read out the words, before we could finally turn them around, focus their attention upon Rachel with her little baton, and start them singing.

When those bell-like voices rang out with "Joy to the World," I thought my heart would positively burst.

TWENTY-FOUR

The fire had burned down to glowing embers by the time Gran stopped talking. Marissa stayed seated by the window, trying not to search the front yard every thirty seconds. The silence was pleasant, complete. They had shared something that went far beyond the story and the words.

Finally Marissa said, "So you and Granpa got married and lived happily ever after."

"Something like that," Gran said, smiling at her. It was not the smile Marissa remembered from before the funeral. This was something new. There was a joining of the soft and welcoming way she had been before Granpa's death with a new depth, a different wisdom. "Colin took quite a while to recover from his illness. I kept postponing my own departure, using his sickness as an excuse. My parents wrote every week, pressing me to set a date for my return. One day, Colin declared it was time to stop pretending he wasn't well in order to keep me from leaving England."

Marissa risked another glance through the front window. The driveway remained as empty as the last time she looked. "And then?"

"Then he proposed to me. And I accepted. Three weeks later, while I was still trying to write the letter telling my parents I wasn't coming home after all, Colin received a letter of his own. The former chaplain of the Arden airbase had become friends with Colin. He had gone home to America and suffered a stroke. He was writing to ask Colin if he would come over and help out.

"Colin's folks were long gone, he was an only child, and did not have any close relatives. The villagers were sorry to see us go, of course, but I was ready to go home. We said it would be just for a year or so, but the Philadelphia church asked Colin to stay on, and we did. And every summer we would go out and visit with our friends in Indiana, and we watched them grow into wonderful adults with families of their own."

"It's a wonderful story, Gran." Marissa tried to put as much feeling as she could into her words. "Thank you for sharing it with me."

"You're welcome, child." Gran cocked her head to one side. "Now can you please tell me why you're either watching the clock or staring out the window?"

"Nothing," Marissa sighed. Two hours late. She felt as if she had been waiting there for years.

"Well, I must say it is wonderful to see you so dressed up." Gran cast an admiring glance over Marissa's freshly washed hair and her white pullover and red plaid skirt. "If I didn't know better, I would say you were completely healed."

"I am much better." She would not try to mask the truth. Not from Gran. Not after everything they had shared. "I just wish I didn't feel so weak."

"That will pass." At the sound of scrunching gravel, Gran raised up to peer over Marissa's shoulder. "Who on earth is that pulling into my drive?"

Marissa looked and squealed and leaped up. "They've come!"

Gran followed her toward the front door. "Who, child?"

"Your Christmas present!" Marissa flung back the door, and waved with both hands over her head as the car flashed its headlights toward her.

Gran joined her at the window and watched the car doors open and two figures tumble out. Laughing, shouting, waving and running down the front walk. "What in heaven's name . . ."

"Merry Christmas!" A dark-haired woman with shimmering black eyes came racing up. She enveloped a tremendously startled Gran in a warm embrace. "Oooh, Andiel Emily, it is so wonderful to see you!"

"We're late, sorry, sorry." The man was tall and square-jawed, and had never lost the last traces of his accent. "But the Indianapolis airport was crazy with snow and people." He reached out his arms, and gave a smile that twisted Marissa's heart. "Hello, Emily. How are you?"

Gran released the dark-haired woman only so she could step toward the man. "Henryk, is it really you?"

"It is indeed." He winked at Marissa over Gran's shoulder. "Hello, my newfound friend."

The woman with the sparkling dark eyes stepped toward Marissa. "You don't remember me, do you?"

"Oh yes, Aunt Annique," Marissa said, accepting the embrace with a grand smile. "I've just been hearing all about you."

Gran looked from one to the other. "But what are you doing here?"

"We're going to sweep you away," Annique said.

"Tomorrow morning at first light," Henryk declared. "We have six hundred miles to cover, and almost a thousand people waiting to greet you."

"Friends and children and grandchildren," Annique agreed merrily.

"Such a circus I can't even imagine," Henryk went on. "It reminds me of the celebration in Arden, before we came to America. But you wouldn't remember that, would you, Emily?"

"Oh, she remembers, all right," Marissa said.

"I can't go anywhere," Gran protested. "Marissa isn't well enough—"

"Look behind you," Henryk said. "A people carrier, that is what they call those things."

"The seats fold down," Annique explained. "We can lay the mattress from your rollaway bed in the back. Marissa can rest and sleep just as much as she likes."

"How did you know about my bed?" Gran focused on Marissa. "You! You planned this!"

Annique's hold on her shoulder tightened. "She is a wonderful young lady, your grandchild."

"Such a time we had," Henryk said around his grin. "First the calls to tell people you could not come, then the calls to say yes, we will gather for Christmas, on New Year's Eve."

"But, but . . ." Gran searched for some protest against the tide of events pulling her along. She said feebly, "Christmas is over and done with."

"Ah, Emily, you will have to do better than that," Henryk said.

Annique smiled at Marissa. There were lines streaming out from her face and eyes, but within the sparkling gaze the pixie could still be found. "Your grandmother gave us the first Christmas of our new lives not three days late, but three months."

"Ach, the young these days," Henryk said, "what do they care of the past?"

"A lot," Marissa said quietly.

Annique smiled her approval, then said, "She taught us two important lessons on that day. First, that the Lord's most wonderful gift knows no season, just as His love knows no bounds."

"I know the other lesson," Marissa declared. She smiled at her grandmother, and said, "When you accept His gift, all is well."

ABOUT THE AUTHOR

DAVIS BUNN is an internationally acclaimed author who has sold more than four million books in fifteen languages. Honored with three Christy Awards for excellence in historical and suspense fiction, his novels include *The Lazarus Trap, Drummer in the Dark,* and bestsellers *Elixir, The Great Divide, Winner Take All, The Meeting Place, The Book of Hours*, and *The Quilt*. A sought-after lecturer in the art of writing, Bunn was named Novelist in Residence at Regent's Park College, Oxford University. Visit his Web site at www.davisbunn.com.